MW00942604

Déjà

Déjà.

Ruby Love Publications
PO Box 1092
Schererville, IN 46375

Printed in the USA

Déjà

Tajana Sutton

Acknowledgments:

First and foremost, I have to give glory to God. I've learned that through him anything is possible. For so long, I wanted to be an Urban Literature Author but I didn't have the courage or pride to see it through. I prayed about it and this is where he led me. I am truly blessed.

To my children Camryn, Victoria, and Kobey, you are my inspiration. You guys keep me on my toes, but I love you very much! To my husband and best friend Toby Lyons, thank you for sticking by my side through the good and the bad. Life has thrown several curveballs at our relationship but here we are still standing tall. I love you very much!

To my mom Victoria Bizzle- McCullough, you are a trooper. I thank you for always being a great mom and supporting me in any decisions that I've made good or bad. For being one of my best friends, but also not letting me forget you're still the mother, I love you! To my father Leroy Sutton, thank you for giving me life, I love you! To my stepfather Ronald McCullough, thank you for your love and support over the years, love you! To my brother Leroy Sutton Jr., I hope that you learn from your mistakes and put

God first in your life he shall see you through, I love you! To my entire family I love you all and I thank you for always supporting me.

A special thanks to my publishing company Enaz Publications. Thank you for believing in my work and taking a chance on me. To my distribution company www.blackbooksplus.com Thank you for all your hard work.

To all my readers thank you for all your love and support. Without you, none of this would be possible. I love you all from the bottom of my heart!

A special thanks to my girl Ms. Lisa Perry. You held me down while my book was still in the works and I love and respect you for that!

For those that I failed to mention, please know that this is just the beginning. If I didn't get you in this one, I will definitely get you in the next one.

Love always,
Tajana S.

~ One ~

"Mom, whose car is that next to Dad's?" asked Déjà as Charlotte pulled into the driveway. Her body jerked forward as Charlotte brought the car to a screeching halt.

When she looked up at her mother, tears were running down her face as she clenched the steering wheel tightly. Charlotte only knew of one person that owned an Audi S8.

"Mommy, why are you crying?"

Charlotte remained silent. She reached into her purse and handed Déjà her cell phone.

"Call 9-1-1."

"Why, is Daddy okay?" Déjà questioned with concern.

"Just do what you're told," Charlotte snapped as she hustled from the car and disappeared inside the house.

Déjà did as she was told, but she wanted to see her daddy. She got out of the car and went into the house.

"9-1-1, what's your emergency?" The female dispatcher asked.

"Um, hi...my name is Déjà Morgan and my mom told me to dial 9-1-1, but I don't know why."

"Is anyone hurt?"

Just as Déjà was about to answer, she was startled by gunshots coming from the upstairs.

"Were those gunshots?" The dispatcher asked.

"Yes, and they came from my mommy and daddy's room," Déjà answered as she began to cry into the phone while tiptoeing up the stairs towards her parent's bedroom.

"Where are you now, honey?"

"Outside my mommy and daddy's room," Déjà answered.

"Do not go in. I'm sending help, just stay with me."

Déjà shrieked when she heard another gunshot from the master bedroom.

"Help is on the way," the dispatcher assured her.

The house was quiet except for Déjà's intense breathing and whimpering. Déjà heard sirens and saw red and blue flashing lights through the big picture window in the loft area where she sat in a fetal position.

"They're here," Déjà said into the phone.

"Okay, stay on the phone until the officers enter the home and get to you," the dispatcher instructed.

The officers burst through the door. Some went upstairs, where she sat shaking and crying hysterically in a corner, others were searching the downstairs area and some were checking the outside premises.

"Clear. Clear. Clear." Anonymous voices blared through the walkie talkie.

"Up here!" shouted a female officer.

She spotted Déjà in a corner across from her parent's bedroom. "Is there anyone else in the house?" questioned the officer.

"My mom and dad are here; I think they're in there," she said, pointing to the master bedroom.

A guy in a gray suit and a policeman in uniform stood on the side of the door to the master bedroom with their guns drawn. The policeman slowly turned the knob and pushed open the door.

"Mommy!" Déjà screamed when she saw Charlotte's body slumped over a chair with a gun in her left hand.

"Get her out of here!" The guy in the gray suit yelled.

"No! I want my mommy!" Déjà screamed.

As the female officer carried her away, Déjà caught a glimpse of her father James and a woman she had seen plenty of times at his office, in the bed. The white sheets were covered in blood.

~ᒎwo~

Déjà was sent to live with her Grandmother Margaret. Margaret was extremely hard on Déjà. She blamed her for what happened that night. She would repeatedly say, "if you were never born, Charlotte would have left that bastard a long time ago."

Déjà despised living there. Margaret often stayed out all night, leaving Déjà in the house by herself. Déjà had become close with her Aunt Gail, who loved kids, but was unable to have children of her own. She didn't like how her mother was treating Déjà, but Margaret wouldn't let Gail take custody of her, because she didn't want to lose the monthly check she was getting from the government after being awarded custody by the state.

When Déjà turned fourteen, she was placed in foster care. DCFS came and removed her from Margaret's home, stating that they had received an anonymous tip that she was being abused.

"I've never laid a finger on Déjà, you bastards!" yelled Margaret as child protective services escorted Déjà to the car.

"Do you have any other family members that you think we should contact?" the woman asked Déjà on the way to the foster home.

"I don't know a lot of my family, but you can try my Auntie Gail," said Déjà.

Gail was ecstatic to take custody of her. She loved Déjà as if she had birthed her.

Margaret was furious when she found out that Gail had custody of Déjà. She approached her at her house.

"You're probably the one that called and said I was abusing her!" She spat, while standing in Gail's living room.

"No I didn't, but I should've because Lord knows you were."

"I've never laid hands on that child, so what would make you think I abused her?"

"You're not supposed to leave no fourteen year old girl in the house by herself for weeks at a time!" Gail shouted.

"She would have to call me to come over and feed her. I'd end up staying over there until you came back from wherever you were."

"When I was fourteen, I stayed in the house by myself," said Margaret.

"Yeah, but I bet it wasn't for weeks at a time with no damn food!" Gail replied with anger.

"You had absolutely nothing in the house for the poor child to eat, not unless she liked eating baking soda. Just admit it, you blame her for what happened to Charlotte and that's not fair to her. Hell, she didn't ask to come into this world. Maybe if you would have stayed in the house with your kids instead of on that damn boat and running the street, you would've known your daughter was sleeping with the son of a pimp, *before* she got pregnant."

Margaret just stood there and stared at Gail. She couldn't respond because she knew that Gail was speaking the truth. Margaret had a gambling habit.

She spent more time on the casino boats than at home raising her children.

Margaret took a seat on the couch with tears in her eyes. She didn't want to accept the fact that her youngest daughter had killed herself over a man. Margaret felt as if she had failed her as a mother.

"I should have been home with you girls teaching y'all the fundamentals of being strong women and not settling for less," Margaret said, crying hysterically. "My baby killed herself because I failed to teach her self-respect. I'm so sorry baby!" she cried out.

"It's okay mom. You made mistakes when we were children, but now is the time to fix it. You have a granddaughter that needs her family right now, so now is the time to make it up to Charlotte," Gail said, calming her mother.

"You're right baby!" said Margaret.

"Déjà will continue to stay here with me, but you need to be active in her life. She has suffered enough," she stated. She hugged and comforted her mother.

Margaret kept her word and helped Gail raise Déjà until she went off to college.

~Three~

At age 18, Déjà enrolled in one of the top colleges in Illinois, majoring in Psychology. She didn't move on campus until her sophomore year. Déjà stood five foot nine with long toned legs, long black hair, and the most beautiful almond shaped eyes. She caught the attention of most of the men on campus, but Déjà only had eyes for one particular guy; Shawn Nelson.

He was a tall, caramel toned brother with a bald head. People often compared him to Teri's boyfriend from the *Soul Food* series. He didn't go to school there, but she'd seen him around quite often. She'd also seen him around her house, but she'd never spoken to him.

Girls would literally fight over him. *He fine, but no man is worth fighting over*, Déjà would say to herself. She knew he was a street dude and that's what turned her on the most. "I'm going to make him my first," Déjà said to her best friend Jade.

Jade was Déjà's roommate and sorority sister in college. They had so much in common. They both had gone through something traumatic in their childhood. For that reason, they understood one another. Jade Rivera was born and raised in Chicago, Illinois. She was the only child of Kate and Reginald Rivera. Reginald was Puerto Rican and Kate was African American.

Jade was yellow skinned, average height, with jet black wavy hair that flowed down her back. She had the most beautiful light brown eyes. Men drooled over her beautiful smile and the one dimple in her right cheek.

Reginald had been convicted of conspiracy to commit murder when Jade was 9-years-old. Kate worked two jobs to make sure Jade never went without electricity, heat, or food on the table. Kate and Reginald agreed not to allow Jade to see her father in prison. He was sentenced to fifteen years without the possibility of parole.

Kate's main objective was to protect Jade from any harm that could possibly come her way. She was one of those parents that always thought of *what if*. She never lived on the first floor of any apartment building, because someone could climb through Jade's window at night; she never allowed men that she dated to come to her home, or meet Jade. No other family members were permitted to look after her other than Kate's mother Cathy. Kate worked as a secretary during the day and at Circuit City in the evening. Jade stayed at her grandmother Cathy's house each day after school until her mother picked her up at night.

One afternoon, when Jade was 13 years old, she was at her Grandmother's house waiting for her mother to get off work. She sat at the kitchen table working on her homework while Cathy baked a cake.

"Oh shucks, I'm out of eggs," Cathy said, looking into the fridge. "I'm going to run up to the grocery store and grab some eggs. Finish your homework and do not open the door for absolutely no one. Your uncle Paul is down in the basement sleeping," she said while putting on her coat.

"Okay, Grandma," Jade said, handing Cathy her scarf.

Cathy walked out the door, locking it behind her. Jade went back and sat at the kitchen table to finish up her homework like she'd been told.

Paul came upstairs from the basement just as Jade was opening her math book.

"Where did Mama go?" He asked, getting a glass out the cabinet.

"She went up the block to the grocery store to get some eggs," Jade said, while pulling out a sheet a paper.

Jade didn't like her Uncle Paul. She felt that he often looked at her in a weird way.

"Why do you have on those tight ass jeans, you're only thirteen?" He said as he brushed past her. He sat down at the table across from Jade.

"My mommy let me wear them, so why do you care what I have on?" she asked with attitude.

"You know you have a smart ass mouth for a little girl."

"Whatever!" she said.

She got up from the table and walked off. She hated the sight of Paul. He was a drunk that forever reeked of alcohol.

"You're not going to keep getting smart with me you little wench!" he said, getting up and going after her.

"Leave me alone!" Jade said, leaving the kitchen.

She went into the living room, sat on the sofa, and picked up the remote off the coffee table.

"Leave you alone? You're in my house, and you're telling me to leave you alone?" He was now standing over Jade.

"Move from in front of the TV. And for the record, this isn't your house. This is Grandma Cathy's house. You're just a drunk that live in her basement!" she replied with attitude.

Jade scooted to the other side of the couch so she could see the television.

"You must think you're grown little girl!" He said, snatching the remote out of her hand and pinning her down on the couch.

"Get off me Uncle Paul," Jade yelled while trying to fight him off.

"I'm going to show you grown," he threatened.

He began kissing her neck while holding her wrists above her head.

"Get off me, please get off of me!" She screamed and cried out.

Kate had just pulled into the driveway and was walking up the walkway when she heard her daughter screaming. She snatched up the *Welcome* mat, retrieving the spare key. She heard more screaming as she unlocked the door. She burst in only to see her oldest brother on top of her daughter. She snapped.

"You motherfucker!" She yelled, charging at him.

Kate picked up the vase that was on the end table closest to the door and smashed it over his head. Paul blacked out, still on top of Jade. Kate rolled him onto the floor and looked over at Jade.

"Did…he?" Kate panted. She tried asking, but couldn't get the words out as she yanked her daughter up, hugging her tightly.

"No, mommy he didn't." Kate was relieved.

Cathy came walking through the door. "Why is my damn door open? Heat is not free!" She fussed.

She closed the door, sat the eggs down on the table, and then removed her coat. She looked at Kate, then at Jade, and then over on the floor at Paul.

"What the hell happened in here?" She said, walking over to Paul who was still knocked out cold on the floor. She glanced at the broken glass on the floor and on the couch. "Who broke my damn vase?"

Paul was now trying to get up off the floor. He sat on the couch with blood pouring down the back of his head onto his shirt.

"I walked in on this motherfucker on top my fucking daughter!" Kate yelled, charging at him once again.

Cathy caught Kate. She looked over at Jade who was balled up on the floor still crying. Her hair was all wild.

"You did WHAT?" she shouted. "You raped that baby?" she screamed.

"I didn't rape nobody," he said.

"That's because I caught you before you could, you sick motherfucker!" Kate yelled, throwing a phone book at him.

"You have lost your damn mind! You are her damn uncle," Cathy yelled at him.

"Fuck y'all," Paul yelled while getting up, and walking toward the front door, but found himself on the floor once again.

He had been hit in the head with the other vase that once sat in the middle of the cocktail table. This time Cathy had thrown it. Paul hasn't been seen since. Cathy said he was on drugs, but he's now in a rehabilitation center. When Reginald heard about the incident, he made a mental note that once he got out he was going to kill Paul.

~ Four ~

Déjà was sitting on her front porch studying and enjoying the summer breeze, when a maroon colored Rivera with extremely dark tint pulled up in front of her house.

"What up Déjà?" Shawn asked, stepping out the car and walking up the walkway.

"Nothing much, what's going on?" she asked, blushing.

"Shit, what are you doing?" he asked, taking a seat on the top stair.

"Studying, I have an exam on Monday."

"Yeah, well I won't disturb you. We can talk later," he said, pulling out his cell phone. "Let me get your number and I'll hit you up a little later."

They exchanged numbers. "I'll call you in a little bit," he said, getting up and heading back toward his car.

Shawn blew the horn as he pulled off playing the *12 Play* album. He called her later that night. After talking on the phone for what seemed like forever, Déjà agreed to go for a ride with him.

He picked her up the following evening around nine.

"Don't get scared, I won't take you out of the area," he said jokingly.

"Yeah, I don't know you like that. You might be a serial killer," she replied with a smile.

They rode around for about an hour. In that hour, Déjà learned that Shawn was twenty three years old, had four siblings, and a four year old daughter. He seemed like a very nice guy.

They began to spend a lot of time together. He would pick her up every day just so they were together. She would ride around with him while he made his rounds and at night, they would catch a movie, go out to eat, or just simply sit and talk. Then either he would drop her back off at home by curfew, or he would rent a room for them. It was that way for about a year, then things began to take a turn for the worse. Déjà and her friend, Ashley, were out at the grocery store when Ashley greeted a girl that was pregnant. The girl looked as if she was about five or six months. Ashley and the pregnant girl spoke for a couple of minutes, before saying their goodbyes. Déjà didn't think anything of it. The following evening, Déjà called Shawn, but his phone rolled over to voicemail. She pressed star, and then entered the access code that Shawn had given her.

You have one new message, to listen to your messages please press one, said the automated system. Déjà listened then pressed one.

"Hey Shawn this is Angel, I met you last night over on 95th Street, give me a call when you get this message," The female voice said.

"What the fuck?" Déjà said to herself.

"Déjà hung up and dialed Shawn's cell phone again, but it kept rolling over to voicemail. He called back about an hour later.

"Hello!" answered Déjà with anger in her voice.

"What up, baby?" he spoke.

"Don't *baby* me. Why aren't you answering your phone?" she asked with attitude.

"Oh, I was on the boat with one of my guys trying to win me some money."

"Whatever! Who is that on your voicemail?"

"I don't know. I haven't listened to my voicemail."

"Well, you have some girl on your voicemail claiming that she met you last night on 95th Street."

He laughed. "I left that message on there, it was an April fool joke!" he said, still laughing. "You think I'm dumb enough to give you my access code and have girls calling?"

"I hope not," she answered, believing him.

"I'm in the area. Can you come outside?"

"Yeah, let me throw on some jogging pants."

"I'll be pulling up in a minute."

"Okay," she replied.

Déjà grabbed her cordless phone and dialed Ashley as she walked out to the driveway. Ashley picked up on the first ring.

"Hey girl, what are you doing?" asked Déjà.

"Girl, I was just about to call you! You're not going to believe this shit!"

"What, what happened?"

"You know that girl that we saw in the grocery store last night, the pregnant chick?" Ashley asked Déjà.

"Yeah, what about her?" Déjà asked as she watched Shawn's car turn on to her block.

"That was Artina. She said that Shawn is the father of her baby!"

"What?" Déjà yelled into the receiver. "You mean to tell me that girl is pregnant by Shawn?"

"Yep, Artina is at my girl Dianna's house right now. I asked Dianna who Artina was pregnant by, and she said a guy name Shawn. I was like Shawn who? She described your Shawn down to his socks."

Déjà was furious. She told Ashley that she would call her back. By the time Shawn pulled up in front of her house, Déjà had smoke coming out her ears. When she walked up to the driver side window, she noticed Shawn had one of his guys in the car with him, but she didn't care. As soon as he rolled down his window and stuck his head out, Déjà words hit him like a ton of bricks.

"You got a girl name Artina pregnant?" Déjà asked.

His entire face turned red. He looked over at his boy, and his boy turned and looked out the window. It was clear he knew the answer to that question.

"That girl ain't pregnant by me," he said, lying through his teeth.

He tried his damnedest to convince her that Artina was lying and that he only had one child.

After pleading that she should believe him, she did. Déjà was so in love with him, she believed that he was telling her the truth, and that everyone else was lying. She just had to learn the hard way. That was only the beginning of his dishonesty and cheating. About a month later, Déjà got a phone call from Artina on her cell phone.

Déjà was furious because she wanted to know who gave out her number. She instantly thought back to her friend Ashley. She was the only mutual person between the two of them. When she spoke to Artina, she learned that Shawn had lied about everything, including his age. He had told her that he was twenty three, but in reality, he was twenty seven. He said that he only had one child, but in fact, had two not including the possibility of the baby Artina was carrying. She also learned that, his four year old daughter was actually nine. Artina told her that Shawn had a live in girlfriend that he had been in a relationship with for the past eight years.

Déjà questioned him about the things that had been told to her. He admitted that most of it was true. He even confessed that there's a strong possibility that the baby Artina was carrying was indeed his. He denied having a live in girlfriend, though. He said he did at one point, but they were no longer together. He said he kept his stash at her crib and that was all. Déjà decided to stay with him because she loved him and honored the fact that he told her the truth instead, of carrying on with his lies. That only lasted a couple months.

One summer afternoon, Déjà and Shawn had gone to a cookout at Gail's house. Déjà noticed her cousin Sharmaine staring at Shawn, but she ignored it. Déjà was just getting out the pool when she noticed that Shawn was no longer outside with the rest of her family. She walked around the front to see if he was up there on his cell phone. She didn't see him. She then went inside the house to see if he had gone to the bathroom. She checked the door knob, but it was locked. She was about to walk away when she heard a woman moaning and the sound of skin smacking. She reached on top of the doorway, and retrieved the key.

She quietly unlocked the door and slowly pushed it open. Déjà went into a state of rage when she saw her cousin Sharmaine bent over the bathroom sink and Shawn behind her banging her brains out. His eyes were shut tightly as if he was on the verge of busting a nut. Sharmaine noticed Déjà standing in the doorway through the reflection in the mirror.

She jumped up, pushing Shawn backwards. Déjà noticed that his dick was covered in her juices as he fell against the tub. Déjà began whooping both his ass and hers. Her Aunt Gail must've heard the commotion because she came running in the bathroom with a frying pan in her hand. She told Shawn and Sharmaine to get the hell out for disrespecting her house.

Déjà was done with Shawn after that, and she was happy about it. She was finally relieved of his bullshit. She had learned more about his deceitfulness after they broke up. He called excessively and would leave threatening messages on her voicemail, but she would just delete them. From that point on, Déjà had sworn off his kind; street dudes.

~ Five ~

After graduating from the University of Illinois with a degree in Business Management, Jade rented an apartment in Hyde Park, one of Chicago's trendiest neighborhoods. She bought herself a Lexus GS 400 and worked as a management consultant in downtown Chicago. She had been dating the love of her life Jayquan Jones a.k.a. Jay for almost three years. He was a street hustler that sold dope by the key. He had a six bedroom home in Olympia Fields, Illinois. He owned three rides: a Mercedes Benz S550, a Lincoln Navigator, and a Range Rover.

A year ago, Jay retired from the dope business as a millionaire. He and his cousin Xavier invested in a nightclub downtown on Michigan Ave. The club was called the *X Spot* which was named after their grandfather Xavier Jones Sr. He was a big time dope dealer that got killed during a deal gone bad. The *X*

Spot was the hottest nightclub in the city. It stayed packed seven days a week.

Friday and Saturday nights were the worst. There were times when people had to wait outside for hours and still couldn't get in. The VIP booths were at all times occupied with the biggest dope dealers in the city, along with athletes and business men. There was a huge one sided mirror over the bar which was Jay's office and another over the lobby which was Xavier's office. They saw everything that went on in their club.

After a long day at the office, Jade decided to head over to the club for a drink. The club was jumping as usual. Everybody and their mamas were in there on this warm spring night. Jade sat at the bar, sipping on her favorite drink, a Cranberry and vodka.

"Get Me Bodied" came on, and the women went crazy. They were sweeping the floor and busting old school dances. Jade's cell phone rang.

"Hey babe," she said, answering, already knowing it was Jay.

"Hey baby, where are you?" he replied, hearing the music in the background.

"I just left the office, but I had a rough day so I came down to the *Spot* for a drink. I thought you would be here, but I didn't see your car out front. Where are you?"

"Actually, I'm sitting outside your apartment. I thought you would have been home by now. If you were having a bad day why didn't you just call me? You know I have my ways of making you feel better," he said in a seductive tone.

"Yes you do!" She said, licking her lips, "but this morning you said you were going to be busy all day, so I didn't want to bother you."

"I'm never too busy for you, baby," he said, reclining the driver's seat.

"I'm leaving the club now, so use your key. I'll be there in about 10-15 minutes. Can you run me a hot bath?" she said, downing the last of her drink.

"Sure thing, baby, see you when you get here," he said as he stepped out the car.

"Okay, I love you!"

"Love you too, beautiful!" he replied.

Jay hit the locks on his Rover and headed for the entrance of Jade's apartment building. When he walked into the lobby, he damn near passed out when he saw his ex-chick Mona. She was sitting in a chair in the corner looking at a magazine. He tried to slip past her before she saw him, but it was too late.

"Hey you, long time no see!" She said, walking toward him.

"Yeah, what are you doing here?" He asked, pressing the up button on the elevator.

"I'm waiting on my girl to come down so we can hit up the club. What about you? You here to see the bitch I been seeing you around town with?" She said, stopping inches from his face.

"That's no longer any of your business," He stepped back to put some space between them.

"Oh, it's like that?" she said with an attitude.

"Yeah trick, it is," he spat. "Why the fuck are you questioning me anyway? Why don't you go question that motherfucker you were fucking in my truck, and get the fuck out my face!" He said as he stepped onto the elevator, letting the doors close in her face.

Jay and Mona had dated five years prior. He had been messing with her for a year, when one day he saw his Range Rover parked in a recreational area near the 35th Street projects. He'd let her use it to go for a job interview, since he and Xavier had to shake a move that day. He told Xavier to pull up next to the truck. He noticed that it was rocking back and forth. He used his extra remote to pop the locks because he'd seen a silhouette of two bodies in the back, through the tint.

He opened the hatchback, startling Mona who was on her hands and knees being fucked doggy style. He snatched both of their asses out the Rover. Xavier beat the shit out of the dude and Jay slapped Mona around a little. He was no woman beater, but he felt Mona was straight up disrespecting him and his shit. They left both Mona and dude out in the freezing cold, half-dressed and shivering. It was seventeen degrees outside. She blew his cell phone up because she knew she would never find another man that would treat her as well as Jay had. He ended up changing his number on her ass. She then got on some dumb shit along with her trifling ass girls.

Jay would come out the club or his house and find his tires slashed, his windows busted on numerous occasions, or she would key his rides. He wasn't able to prove that it was her, but he knew it was. When asked, of course she would deny it. But he warned her that if he ever caught her, he was going to put a slug in her head.

When Jade came in, Jay was sitting on the couch flipping through the channels. "Cable is a waste of money," he said, tossing the remote on the cocktail table.

"I agree!" said Jade, leaning over and giving him a peck on the lips.

He grabbed her by the waist and pulled her down on his lap.

"I missed you!" he said, tonguing her down.

"Did you really? Show me!" She said, pulling her blouse over her head and straddling him.

Jay removed his shirt as well. He began sucking on her firm nipples. He stuck his hand under her skirt and began playing with her clit, then inserted his index finger deep inside her wet pussy, causing her to moan.

She unzipped his pants, and out sprung a nine inch hard on. She got down on her knees and took all nine inches in her mouth. He gasped for air. If Jade couldn't do anything else, she definitely knew how to make her man feel good. He was on the verge of cumming when she straddled him once again.

She slid down inch by inch, until her soaking wet pussy swallowed all nine inches. She rode him until her body began to tremble. He turned her over on her knees and hit her from the back. He found her g-spot in no time, and banged into it. Jade was now biting down on the couch pillow.

"Pull…out…babe…you're…not…wearing…a…a! " She said, trying to stop him, but it was too late. He had exploded deep inside her. He flopped down on the couch. She rested her head on his chest.

"Why didn't you pull out?"

"I'm sorry baby. It was feeling too good," he said still trembling.

"I hope I don't get pregnant," she said, trying to get up, but he pulled her back down.

"Why, you don't want to have my baby?" He questioned, while kissing her on the lips.

"We're not married. Plus, I'm not feeling the whole baby daddy thing," Jade said, kissing him back.

"Neither am I. You're going to be my wife."

"Yeah, we'll see," She said, getting up and walking toward the bedroom.

"That we will," He followed closely behind her, ready for round two.

~ *Six* ~

"The X *Spot* is one of the hottest nightclubs in the Chi," explained Jade, trying to convince Déjà to go out with her.

Déjà wasn't into clubs, so she hardly ever went. Besides, she was exhausted. She had a very busy week at the office, and still had paperwork piled up on her desk in her home office. But, she hadn't been out with her best friend in a very long time, so she finally agreed.

"Let me find something to wear. What time are you picking me up?"

"I'll be there at ten," answered Jade.

"Cool, I'll be downstairs, so do not keep me waiting."

"You don't keep *me* waiting!" mocked Jade.

Déjà looked at the clock on the microwave. It read: 4:26. "I got time to take a short nap," she said as she stepped out of her dress pants.

As soon as she got comfortable under the comforter, the phone rang. She considered letting it roll over to voicemail, but decided against it.

"Hello!" She answered in a sleepy tone.

"Hello, may I speak to Déjà?" said the unfamiliar male voice.

"This is she, who is this?" asked Déjà.

"This is Xavier."

"Who?"

"Xavier. Your girl Jade gave me your number the other day."

"Oh, did she? She never mentioned that to me."

"I told her not to. I wanted to get at you myself?"

"What!" she asked in an irritated tone.

"Calm down baby, Jade mess with my cousin Jay, so I've seen you around the way a few times. I told her to hook a brotha up. She handed me your number, and told me to hook myself up!" he said, laughing.

"That sounds like something Jade would do, but how I know you're not making this up?"

"You just said that sounds like something your girl would do!" he said sarcastically. "But check it, I hear your girl will be at the *Spot* tonight. Are you coming?"

"I was, but now I don't know!" she said, playing hard to get.

"Aw, don't be like that, baby."

"I'm not your *baby*."

"Oh, but you will be!" said Xavier with confidence.

"Whatever! I'm going to try to get a nap in before I have to get showered and dressed to kill Jade for giving out my number without my permission."

"Cool, I'll let you catch some z's. But, I'll see you later, right?"

"Sure. Whatever!" she said with a yawn.

"Don't be so mean, baby!"

"Why do you insist on calling me *baby*? I'm not your *baby*. I don't even know you!"

"You will, and you're going to love every minute of it."

"Really?"

"Yes, really!"

"Okay dude! I'm going to sleep now. I'll talk to you later," she said before hanging up, rolling over, and falling asleep.

———————

Beep…Beep…Beep sounded the alarm clock. Déjà reached over, and hit the snooze button. It was now 6:30pm. She went over to the closet to find something to wear to the club. She was not too happy about Jade giving a complete stranger her phone number, but was thrilled at the same time. *I'm tired of buying batteries for that damn 'Jack Rabbit'!* She thought to

39

herself. Déjà hadn't had any real dick since Shawn, but that was because she had only been approached by thuggish dudes, and she'd sworn off those kinds of men for good. After trying on damn near every outfit she owned, Déjà finally decided on a black and gold BP cut out dolman sleeve top, a pair of black shiny cinched leggings, and a pair of BP wedges.

Déjà warmed up and ate some left over pasta before hitting the shower.

"There's nothing like drinking on an empty stomach," she said to herself.

As Déjà sat at the table stuffing her face, she thought back to the phone call she had received earlier from Xavier. The name sounded very familiar, but she couldn't pin point where she'd heard it. Déjà looked up at the clock, and noticed it was already 7:45. She showered, then started on her hair. She took her ponytail out and went over her thick long black hair with some *Golden Hot* flat irons, applied her MK makeup, and then got dressed. Déjà checked herself out in the full length mirror.

"Damn, I have to admit, I'm looking damn good!" she said, adjusting her blouse. The leggings exposed her curves, her hair hung beautifully down her backside, and her makeup was flawless.

––––––––––––

"Who the hell is Xavier, and why did you give him my phone number without checking with me first?" Déjà said to Jade as soon as they hooked up that evening.

"Before you snap, he had been begging me to introduce him to you, since that day you dropped me off over Jay parents' house about 2 weeks ago. He was sitting in the white Range Rover.

"Still, why didn't you tell me about him first? He just called, and I had no clue as to who the hell he was."

"Because I know you; you would have come up with any reason as to why you couldn't holla at him."

"Is there a reason why I shouldn't?" Déjà asked.

"No. He is the kind of man that you have sworn off, but he is nothing like Shawn punk's ass."

"And how do you know that?"

"One, Xavier and Jay are cousins; they both used to be big time dope dealers, but are now retired. Two, because I've seen him in a Navigator, a Benz, and a Range Rover, and not to mention he's part owner of the club we're going to tonight. Plus, he owns other businesses. He stay iced out and laced in the finest gear, that's how I know!"

"That's where I recognize that name! He was a big time dope dealer. He was the guy that Shawn would go see to re-cop on his product," Déjà said. "You gave my number to a drug dealer?" Déjà asked agitated.

"Didn't I say he is retired from the game? Besides, haven't you ever heard of the saying *don't judge a book by its cover?*"

"Isn't that what you're doing? Hell he might be a serial killer. Besides, you know I can't get into a relationship with another damn dope dealer. You know my history with Shawn. I said I will never do that brand of men again. Now I have to change my number!" she spat.

"He's going to be at the club tonight, so do you still want to go?" Jade asked, hoping Déjà wouldn't say no. She didn't want her outfit to go to waste.

"Girl please, I'm looking too good to go back home!" Déjà said, slapping five with her best friend.

~ Seven ~

The club was off the chain. Déjà and Jade headed straight for the dance floor as Bey called for all the "Single Ladies." They tore up the dance floor, but Déjà felt as if she was being stared at. They took a seat over at the bar. Déjà ordered an Amaretto Stone Sour and Jade ordered a Cranberry and vodka.

The bartender came over with their drinks. "These are for you pretty lady, and the drinks are on the house," he said, handing Déjà a dozen red roses.

"I think you have the wrong girl," Déjà said to the bartender."

"Is your name Déjà?"

"Yes."

"Well, I have the right girl."

"Who sent these?" she asked, smelling the flowers.

"Read the card," he said with a smile.

Déjà looked over at Jade. She had a big joker smile plastered on her face. She opened the envelope and pulled out the card. It read: *Save me a dance, beautiful!*

"Roses and he don't even know you? Now that's what I'm talking about!" said Jade.

"Okay, I must admit that was sweet, but I had my share of drug dealers and nothing good came out the relationship. There was cheating; baby mama drama, bonding them out of jail, etc. I just can't tolerate another street dude," Déjà said to Jade while sipping on her drink.

"All men have those problems, not just street dudes."

"I know, but they're most likely to come with that bullshit."

"Says who?"

"Says me!"

"Slow Dance" by R. Kelly came blasting through the speakers. "This here song is a special one from my main man Xavier," the DJ said, lowering the music.

Déjà looked over at Jade. She was smiling from ear to ear. Jay walked up behind Jade and kissed her on the cheek.

"Hey baby, can I have this dance?" Jay asked, reaching out for Jade's hand.

Jade was about to decline because she didn't want to leave Déjà by herself.

"Go head girl!" Déjà said to her best friend.

Déjà was sipping on her drink when she felt a tap on her shoulder.

"Can I have this dance?" A male's voice spoke into her left ear.

She turned around to decline his request, but she just stared at what was standing in front of her.

Xavier was a tall, brown skinned brother with a low hair cut that was full of waves. He was sporting a muscle shirt that complemented his upper body, and a crisp pair of slacks.

"I told you I'm going to make you mine!" he said as he took Déjà's hand and led the way to the dance floor.

He whispered charming things in her ear the entire time they danced. Déjà hated to admit it, but Xavier had her panties soaked.

"I need to go to the ladies room," Déjà said, stepping back.

"Okay, I'll be at the bar," he said with a grin on his face, showing off his gorgeous smile.

Déjà couldn't stop blushing. *There is something about this man that's attracting my attention*, she thought. Déjà had promised herself that she would never do another drug dealer, but Xavier was a gentleman.

She pondered whether she should slip out the back door or not, but it seems that he had the place on lock. There was a big muscular guy sitting on a stool next to the back door. He smiled and nodded at Déjà, as if he knew her. Women were looking her up and down with envy in their eyes. One particular girl stared at Déjà with her nose turned up, but Déjà paid her no mind. Men that were trying to get at her before, now turned in the other direction, and the DJ followed Xavier's every command. Plus, she rode with Jade, so she had no choice but to go back to the bar.

"I'm glad you didn't run out the backdoor," Xavier said with an attractive smile.

"There's a back door?" she said, jokingly.

"Jokes, I like that!"

"Yeah, what else do you like?"

"You, and I hope the feelings are mutual."

"I'm going to be honest. I've dated your kind and have nothing good to say about it, so I'm not sure how to feel."

"My kind, what exactly is my kind?"

"The kind that doesn't punch a time clock," she said.

"Oh! Gotcha, I can respect that. Your girl told me a little about your past. But know this; that was my hustle, but it does not define me as a man. You can't compare me to guys that you dated in the past. A man's occupation has nothing to do with how he treats a woman. But let me ask you this, what kind of bad experiences did you have?" he asked curiously.

"Oh, let's see! There was cheating, baby mama drama, jail time, and having to bond them out of jail. You know, shit like that."

"My point exactly, that's just the type of dude they were. That has nothing to do with what they do for a living. If they drove a milk truck, they will still do the same thing because that's their personality. As far as jail and you bonding me out, that's something you will never have to worry about. Trust me!"

"Why should I trust you?" Déjà said with a smile.

"I just told you, I'm not that dude you used to know. I'm *one of a kind*, baby!" he said with self-assurance.

"Okay, Mr. *one of a kind*, can you at least enlighten me on your government name?"

"It's Xavier Jones."

"Okay, Mr. Jones. I'm Déjà Morgan."

Déjà and Xavier talked a little longer, until they were interrupted by a short, light skinned brother with braids.

"Yo X, we have a problem," he said in a whisper.

Xavier looked over at Déjà.

"Go ahead, I'm about to get out of here anyway."

"Can I call you tonight?" he asked.

"Sure."

"Alright, baby. Tell your girl I owe her one," he said, kissing her on the cheek.

On the way home, Jade grilled Déjà about her conversation with Xavier. "You know I got to be nosey, right?" Jade said. "I saw y'all smiling all in each other faces. What did y'all talk about?"

"Now you're spying on me?" she said with a smirk.

"You know I had to watch him just in case he tried something slick. Then I'd have to cut him."

"He seems like a really nice guy. Not to mention, he is drop dead gorgeous with a body to match."

"He is fine girl. You're lucky I didn't get to him first," she said teasingly.

"You did, remember?" Déjà said.

"Yeah, but he's checking for you."

They laughed as Jade pulled up in front of Déjà's apartment building. It was three in the morning, and Déjà was exhausted.

———————

As soon as she walked in, she put the roses in water, ran a hot bath, and added her favorite Victoria Secret fragrance *Love Spell* with a few floating candles. She undressed, and then pulled her hair up into a ponytail. She stepped into the steamy hot water. It worked wonders on her aching body. She couldn't get

Xavier off her mind. She laid back, fantasizing about making love to him. Just as she was getting deep into thought, the phone rang. Déjà got out the tub to get it, but she didn't make it in time.

The voicemail light blinked. Déjà slipped into her pajamas, turned on the television, but turned down the volume, then checked her voicemail.

Hey baby, this is Xavier. I told you I was going to call you tonight, and I don't make promises I don't intend on keeping. Also, I wanted to make sure you made it home safe. Give me a call when you get this message, one.

Déjà didn't notice how sexy his voice was until then. She listened to his message over and over again. She didn't want to come off as desperate, so she sent a text message instead of calling. It read:

Hey Xavier, it's Déjà. I was in the tub when you called, but I did listen to your voice message. Thanks for making me feel special tonight. I really enjoyed your company. I am extremely tired, so is it ok if we talk tomorrow?

He replied: *That was nothing baby, you'll see. Get some rest. I'll call you tomorrow.*

~ Eight ~

Jade called early the following morning.

"I knew I should have turned my ringer off before I went to sleep," Déjà mumbled under her breath.

"Hey girl, what are you doing?" Jade said in an energized tone.

"You must've forgot that I was out all night with you, so what do you think I'm doing? Sleep!" she said, answering her own question.

Just as Déjà was about to tear Jade a new asshole, her other line beeped. "Hold on, my other line is beeping."

She clicked over. "Hello!" she said in an irritated tone.

"Hey, baby, it's Xavier. Did I wake you?"

"No, actually Jade did."

"Oh okay. How long will it take you to get dressed?"

"Um, about an hour, why?" She asked.

"It's a surprise. No jeans or gym shoes. Where do you live?"

Déjà gave him her address, and then ended the call. She got up to shower, but forgot that Jade was on the other line. The phone rang back. She let it ring. It was eighty-five degrees outside, so she decided to pull her hair back into a ponytail. She wore a satin halter jumpsuit and a pair of sandals with a four inch heel. Her cell phone chimed just as she was putting the finishing touches on her makeup.

"Hello," she answered.

"I'm downstairs in the lobby," Xavier said.

"I'll be right down."

"Cool."

She applied her strawberry lip gloss, set the alarm, and headed toward the elevator. Xavier greeted her with a dozen red, pink, and white roses and a kiss on the cheek.

"You look good, baby!" he said.

"So do you," she replied. He was wearing a black designer button up, a pair of black slacks and a pair of gators. He opened the passenger side door of his white Mercedes Benz S550 with white rims and a double sunroof.

"So where are you taking me?" She asked as they merged onto Lake Shore Drive.

"I told you, it's a surprise. So, tell me a little about yourself," he said with a smile.

"Well, to make a long story short, I'm 25 years old. I went to Flowers High School, and graduated with a degree in Psychology from the University of Illinois. I now work as a social worker. What about you?" She asked, looking over at him.

"I'm 29, I was born and raised here in Chicago, I graduated from Prosser High School, and I have a degree in business from Purdue University." Déjà was shocked.

"What you didn't think I was educated?" he asked with a smile.

"If you went to college, why were you selling drugs?" she asked.

"I didn't have a choice, couldn't find work. I turned to the streets and got caught up. I became a drug dealer, and now I'm retired from the game, so glad I am!"

"Was it really that bad?"

"If you only knew," he said, "that shit is a headache, not to mention, dangerous as hell. To be honest with you, I didn't think I would ever make it out the game alive or not in the joint."

"I don't see how you can risk your life like that for a dollar."

"Trust me when I tell you, baby, I made more than a dollar," he laughed.

"Have you ever been locked up?"

"They tried to get us, but the cases never stuck. We had to deal with motherfuckers in the streets that wanted our seat on the throne, and that was just as bad!"

"So you're no longer a drug dealer?" Déjà asked, wanting to hear it from his mouth."

"No, not anymore!" he replied.

"So, what is it that you do with your spare time?"

"I own a few homes, a couple of rental properties, a barbershop/beauty salon, a nightclub and I have a 5-year-old son named Jeremiah. I wouldn't necessarily say I have a lot of spare time."

"I guess not! Have you ever been married?" she asked.

"No, never married. I was too deep into the streets to settle down," he said as he exited Lake Shore Drive."

Déjà and Xavier talked and laughed until they pulled into the parking garage of Navy Pier.

"I love this place! My Aunt Gail used to bring me here as a kid," said Déjà on the verge of tears. She hated to think back to her childhood. It was filled with so much despair.

"This is just the beginning. I have a whole day planned for you," said Xavier, hearing the hurt in her voice.

He knew she had gone through something tragic in her childhood from the look in her eyes, but thought it was too soon to ask.

They walked the Pier hand and hand until they reached *Midnight*. *Midnight* was one the most talked about cruise ships that sailed Lake Michigan. Before boarding the boat, they stopped to take a picture together, then headed inside. They grabbed a table next to the window. Xavier had reserved the entire section so that no one will be seated near them as they got to know each other.

"How did you know this was my favorite place?" asked Déjà.

"I did my homework," Xavier said, winking at her. She just stared at him with a smile.

They both ordered the salmon dinner and a few desserts from the dessert table. The band was playing "Here and Now" by Luther Vandross.

"May I have this dance?" asked Xavier, taking Déjà's hand and leading her to the dance floor.

He wrapped his arms around her waist and pulled her in close to him. Déjà felt what seemed like ten inches bulging out his pants. When she looked up at him, he was smiling hard.

"I'm turning you on!" he said, looking down at her breasts.

"How do you know that?"

"Your nipples just told me!" he said sarcastically.

Déjà looked down at her nipples and they were hard as rocks. They both laughed.

Déjà was really feeling Xavier. She couldn't wait to get a taste of him. They were damn near having sex on the dance floor. By the time the boat docked, Déjà was horny as shit.

"Will you spend the night with me?" he asked, hoping she would agree.

"Don't you think it's a little too soon for me to be spending the night with you?" She asked, playing hard to get.

"No, I don't. What, are you scared?" Xavier said in a cocky tone.

"Should I be?"

"No!"

"How do I know you're not one of those guys that just like to hit it and quit it?" she said with a smirk.

"Who said anything about hitting it?" He said with a grin plastered on his face. They chuckled.

Truth be told, she wanted him to tear it up. Déjà hadn't had any dick in over a year. She was feeling like a crack head in rehab, but she didn't want him to know that. But, if he did his homework like he claimed he had, he would already know. Déjà and Xavier stopped by the picture booth. He purchased two photos that they had taken before going on the boat. They walked around the Pier for hours, and then took a ride up Lake Shore Drive with the sunroof open. He merged back onto 80/94.

"Would you like to go see a movie?"

"Sure!"

"Have you ever been here?" asked Xavier, pulling into a parking spot.

"No I'm afraid not," Déjà answered.

"It's the bomb!" he said, helping her out the passenger seat.

Déjà was impressed. She had never seen a movie theater quite like this one. This place served dinner doing the movie; had a bartender serving drinks, and the most comfortable seats. They agreed on Jamie's new movie.

"You never answered my question," he said.

"What was the question?" Déjà asked, knowing exactly what question he was referring to.

"Will you spend the night with me?"

"I would have to go home for an overnight bag."

"We can stop by Macy's and you can get whatever you need."

"You really did do your homework didn't you? That's my favorite store."

He smiled.

After the show, they swung by Macy's. Xavier bought her some sexy lingerie, a jean jumpsuit that she had been wanting, a pair of designer heels with a matching handbag along with some under garments. They arrived at Xavier's house at a little past ten. Xavier's home was absolutely stunning. It was a two story residence with five bedrooms, four baths and a huge kitchen with all stainless steel appliances. The living room had all white furniture with plush white carpet and a sixty-five inch plasma mounted on the wall.

"Your home is beautiful!" Déjà said, impressed.

"Thank you, make yourself at home. The remote to the plasma is on the table. You can choose a movie that you wouldn't mind watching," said Xavier, disappearing into the kitchen.

Déjà browsed through his movie collection and came up on a wide selection of porn. "We can watch one of those if you like," Xavier said, sneaking up behind her.

"Are you trying to give me a hint?"

"I'm not going to lie, I crave you. But, I'm following your lead. You were just paying extra attention to the porn, so I figured you wanted to watch one!" he said, teasing.

"You crave me, huh?"

"You know I do. You felt my dick when we were on the dance floor."

"Yes I did!" She said, licking her lips.

Seeing her gesture turned him on. "Whenever you ready baby," Xavier stated as he turned and disappeared back into the kitchen.

He returned with two champagne glasses and a bottle of champagne. He put on the movie she chose which was "The Kingdom" and poured them both a glass of champagne.

Déjà took a few sips while watching him take off his shirt. That alone had her moist. He had a body similar to Michael Jai White. He lay down on the couch, pulling Déjà down on top of him.

He held her tight as she relaxed her head on his chest. Fifteen minutes into the movie, they both had dozed off.

Déjà woke up in a cold sweat from yet another bad dream. He must've felt her jump because he woke up with a look of worry on his face.

"Are you okay?" he asked.

"Yeah, I'm fine. Where is your restroom?" Déjà asked with tears welling up in her eyes.

"Down the hall, first door on your right," he said.

Déjà went into the bathroom to try to shake off another one of those dreams she'd occasionally have of that awful night when she was just ten years old. She splashed water on her face and applied some more lip gloss. When she returned to the living room, Xavier stood up with his hand out. He led her upstairs and into the master bedroom. The room was almost the size of Déjà's entire apartment. The room had a king size canopy bed, a sitting area, a fireplace in one corner, and a huge fish tank in the other. He led her over to the sitting area.

"Have a seat," he demanded. He went into the master bathroom and ran her a tub of water in the Jacuzzi then re-entered the bedroom.

"So are you going to tell me what that was all about?" he asked, taking a seat next to her on the sofa.

"Long story," Déjà answered with her head hung, and not wanting to talk about it.

"I have nothing but time," he said, lifting her head.

"It was a dreadful dream that I have every now and again of something that happened when I was ten. But I really don't want to talk about it right now," she said in a low tone of voice.

"Okay, whenever you ready to tell me, I'm ready to listen."

She'd never had a man to care about her feelings. Her heart became heavy. "Thanks. You know, you don't seem like the typical street guy," Déjà said, trying to change the subject.

"I try not to mix business with pleasure. Don't get me wrong, I have my share of issues, but I'll try not to bring that into your world," he said, hugging her.

"I ran you a bubble bath with your favorite scent, *Love Spell.* I'm going to take a shower," he said as he began taking off his pants.

"Are you afraid to bathe with me, and how did you know I like *Love Spell*?" she asked, going over to him.

"I told you. I did my homework and I was trying to give you your space, but if you want me to bathe with you, then you got that. I didn't want to scare you off," he said, kissing her on the forehead.

"Scare me off? Ain't nobody scared of you!" she said with a laugh. They walked into the bathroom.

"You talk a lot of shit. For your sake, you better be able to back it up," he said, kissing her. He pried her lips apart and slipped her the tongue.

"Oh, I just hope you ain't no damn minute man," she said, not being able to hold back any longer.

"Now that's funny!" he said, walking toward the Jacuzzi.

They both stripped down to their birthday suits and were impressed. *I knew he was fine, but damn. My prediction was right. He is about nine and a half inches, and its thick,* Déjà thought to herself as she stared at his package. Because it had been over a year since Déjà last had some, she was beyond nervous, but she wasn't going to let him know that, especially after all the shit she had talked. But she didn't have to, her expression told it all.

"You're not talking shit anymore, I see. You petrified now, huh?" he asked with a devilish grin.

"You have the package, but let's see what you can do with it," she said still trying to hold her ground.

Déjà and Xavier stepped into the hot tub. The jets felt good on her body. He pulled her over to him. She straddled him as he began sucking on her rock hard nipples. She was grinding on his rock hard dick. She wanted him inside of her so bad she could taste it, yet he insisted on teasing her.

"So you're going to tease me?" she said through whimpers.

"Yep that's the plan!" he said while tongue kissing her neck. Déjà was about to explode when he began washing her body. He lifted her out the tub, dried her off, and took her over to the bed.

"You ready!" he said, spreading her legs.

"Take it easy. It's been a while," she said, rubbing his shaft.

Her body quivered as he kissed her leg, working his way up her thigh, nearing her clitoris. He kissed around her clit. His hot tongue then licked her opening causing her to scream out in ecstasy. She never had a man to go down on her before, so this made her literally climb the wall.

"I can't take it, baby," she said, trying to close her legs.

"I'm just getting started baby!" he said now sucking on her clitoris.

"I'm…about…to…cuuummmm!" Tears came down her face as her body vibrated.

"You want me to stop?" he said, looking up at her.

"No. Just promise me you won't hurt me," she said.

"I promise, baby. I'm all yours!" he said as he dug all nine and a half inches deep inside her.

He had to start off slow, because she was tight. She screamed out in ecstasy as he dug in deeper, touching down on her g-spot. She tried scooting away, but he held her tight in position. She came again and again as he pounded against her g-spot. He held her body firmly against his as they came together. She fell right to sleep in his arms.

———————

She woke up the following morning to gentle kisses on her back. She looked over at the clock on the nightstand. It was 10:06. She turned toward Xavier and tongued him down.

"So are you going to give me a chance to show you what the good life is like?" He asked while rubbing between her legs.

"Do I have a choice?" she asked, spreading her legs.

"You always have a choice, baby, but I'm hoping you say yes," he said, climbing on top of her.

"Okay, yes," she said, allowing him to enter her once again.

They went at it again, then Xavier made her cum three more times before he made her bacon, eggs, and pancakes with fresh squeezed orange juice for breakfast.

"I have to make a run. Do you want to stay here, or do you want me to take you home?" He asked as he cleared the table.

"I need to get home and do some paperwork, so you can take me home," she said going back upstairs to shower and get dressed.

As soon as Déjà walked through the door, her phone began ringing off the hook. She let it go to voicemail, but whoever it was called consistently.

"Hello."

"Where the hell have you been?" Jade shouted into the phone.

"You wouldn't believe it if I told you," Déjà replied as she thought back to her rendezvous.

"Try me! You put me on hold yesterday morning, and I haven't heard from you since."

"I'm sorry girl. That was Xavier on the other line when I told you to hold on."

"Aw, shit. Let me take a seat. I got to hear this!" Déjà filled Jade in on everything from the time he picked her up to him dropping her off this morning.

She was practically screaming through the phone. "I'm so happy for you!" she said with excitement.

"Thanks girl. He is a really nice guy and the sex was off the chain. I'm going to take a nap now. Can I call you back later?"

"A'ight girl, I'll talk to you later."

~Nine~

Jade had just arrived home from a long day at the office. She stopped and grabbed the mail then talked to the security guard, Sheena for a few minutes. As Jade turned the corner, heading for the elevator, she was damn near knocked down by a high yellow chick with fire red hair. The woman looked familiar, but she couldn't pin point where she had seen her face.

"Excuse you!" said Jade.

"No excuse you!" the yellow chick said in a nasty tone then walked away.

Jade got on the elevator and pressed the number five. She was searching through her purse for her keys as she exited the elevator. She turned the corner and damn near fainted when she saw 'BITCH' spray painted on her door. Jade stared at the door for a minute, and then it hit her.

"Dumb bitch!" she yelled, remembering who the yellow broad was. That was Jay's ex-girlfriend Mona.

Jade went into the apartment, threw her purse down, and dialed Jay's cell.

"Hey beautiful," said Jay, picking up on the first ring.

"Don't *hey beautiful* me. You need to get your ass over here and get this damn spray paint off my damn door since you can't control your women!" she yelled while slipping on some jogging pants.

"What are you talking about Jade?" He asked, jumping out his office chair.

"I'm talking about your high yellow ass ex-girlfriend spray painting *bitch* on my damn door!" yelled Jade, now fuming.

"How you know it was her?" He asked as he grabbed his jacket and stepped onto the elevator.

"Because the silly bitch damn near knocked me down when I was on my way up here. It didn't click in that it was her until I seen that shit on my door.

But, I'm hoping the bitch is still down there," she said, slipping her t-shirt over her head.

"No, baby, I'm on my way. Just stay in the apartment," said Jay while practically running to his car.

"Like hell! By the time you make it here. That bitch will be on a stretcher," Jade said, walking out the front door and slamming it. She banged on the down button on the elevator.

"Okay, baby, just calm down," he said, putting the pedal to the metal.

"Calm down!" Jade yelled before hanging up the phone on him.

Jade couldn't get to the first floor fast enough. As soon as the elevator doors opened she ran into the main lobby. No one was there but Sheena.

"Hey, have you seen this high yellow bitch with a head full of red weave?" she asked Sheena."

"I know exactly who you're talking about, but she gone," Sheena said, getting up from her desk.

"Damn!" said Jade, looking out the front door.

"What's going on girl?" Sheena asked, emerging from behind her desk.

"That hoe spray painted *bitch* on my damn door."

"What? I had a feeling that trick was up to no good," said Sheena.

"It's cool, I'll catch her, and when I do, it's going to take the jaws-of-life to get me off of her," Jade said to Sheena.

"What beef you got with her?" Sheena asked.

"I don't even know the broad. She used to mess with Jay, and is now pissed because I got him on lock," she said, taking a seat in a chair.

"You know I don't understand why women take their frustrations out on the woman instead of the man," said Sheena.

"I know right, just ignorant!"

"Did you call Jay?"

"Of course I did, who you think going to remove that shit off my door? Sure as hell ain't gonna be me. I wasn't fucking her!" She said, getting out of her seat.

"Well go on back upstairs, girl. I'll make sure it doesn't happen again, and I'll be sure the other security guards know not to allow her on the premises," Sheena said as she walked back over to her desk.

"A'ight, thanks Sheena," Jade said as she stood up and headed toward the elevator.

Jade walked back into her apartment and instantly became nauseous. She ran to the bathroom. She heard the door open and close.

"Baby," shouted Jay.

"I'm in here," she replied, still hovered over the toilet. Seconds later, he appeared in the doorway of the bathroom.

"What's the matter?" he asked.

"I'm nauseous that's all. I think it's that Chinese food I ate for lunch."

"You always eat Chinese food and it has never made you sick before."

"Well maybe my stomach didn't agree with it today."

"Naw, that's not what it is," he said with a smile.

He knew exactly what it was, and was happy about it.

"Okay, Dr. Jay, if that's not it, what is it then?"

"You're pregnant," he said, helping her up off the floor.

"No I'm not, Jay."

"Okay, then why is it that when we were having sex the other night you wouldn't let me go all the way in?"

"It was hurting, that's why. But that doesn't mean anything."

"Yes it does. It means that your cervix is closed."

"Cervix, what you know about a cervix?"

"I'm not stupid Jade, I did graduate from college. I know that when you're pregnant your cervix closes."

"I don't even know anything about that, so how do you?"

"I've read up on child birth. I've always wanted a couple of kids and I'm hoping you'll be the woman to give them to me."

"It definitely won't be me if you don't learn to control your hoes, and keep them the fuck away from my front door," she warned.

"I will deal with her, baby, but in the meantime I'm going to run up to the store and get some paint so that I can get that bullshit off your door."

"Now that's a good idea!" she stated sarcastically.

"Whatever, Jade!" he said, kissing her on the cheek. "Do you need me to bring you back anything?"

"Yeah, a baseball bat, because if she come here again, I'm busting her shit wide open."

"You're not going to be out there fighting."

"Okay, let me catch that bitch in this building again!"

"I'll be right back, Jade," he said, walking out the door.

I'm fucking Mona ass up on sight, he thought as he rode the elevator back down to the first floor.

———————

Jade's cycle was two days late. About a week later, she set up an appointment with her doctor because she hadn't been feeling good lately. She'd been throwing up, had the chills, and cramping.

"What time is your appointment, baby?" Jay asked.

"At three o' clock," she said, feeling like she was about to vomit again.

"Okay, I'm downstairs. I'm going to come up and shower then I'll take you," he said, getting out the car.

"You can come take a shower, but I can go to the doctor by myself."

"Why you don't want me to go with you?" he asked

"Because you been out at the club all night. Aren't you tired?" she said, hoping he would say yes.

"I own the club. All I do is sit in a chair. Besides, I want to know what's going on with you. Although, I already know," he said, walking through the door and hanging up the phone.

"Why do you think I'm pregnant?" She said, laying her head back on the sofa.

He greeted her with a forehead kiss.

"Trust me, I know, baby, but give me about 15 minutes to shower, then I'll take you to the doctor so they can confirm my assumption," he said, heading toward the bathroom.

"Whatever!" she said, lying down.

~ *Ten* ~

Déjà woke up around 10:30pm. She prepared some baked chicken breast, rice medley, and string beans then checked her voicemail. She had turned the ringer off before taking a nap, so she could get some uninterrupted sleep for a change. She had no messages. She turned on the news. The newscaster was reporting a shooting at a local night club.

"See, that's why I don't do clubs!" Déjà said to herself.

She worked on some of the paperwork that had been piling up on her desk, took a bath, and was back in bed by 2am. Just as Déjà was getting relaxed under the comforter, she heard a knock at the door.

"I'm going to kill Jade for coming here this late. She knows I have to be at work early in the morning," she said tying her robe as she walked toward the front door.

Déjà looked through the peep hole.

"Oh, shit!" she said, fixing her ponytail. When she opened the door, Xavier stood there with tears falling down his cheeks.

"What's wrong?" She asked with concern.

"They shot him, baby!" he said with anger.

"Come in Xavier. Who shot who?" Déjà asked, pulling him into the apartment.

He plopped down on the couch with his hands folded on top of his head. "What are you talking about Xavier, who shot who?" she asked again, sitting next to him, and rubbing his leg.

"My lil' brother, they shot my brother. Those motherfuckers shot my damn brother!" he yelled, slapping Déjà's lamp, causing it to fly across the room.

He stood up and began pacing the floor. She went over and hugged him. He held her tight. Déjà didn't want to question him. She just wanted him to calm down. Déjà guided him back over to the couch.

"I'm sorry, baby. This is not your problem," he said, wiping his tears away.

"What do you mean, you are mine now, remember? That means that from now on, your problems are my problems. Whenever you need me, I'm here," said Déjà, hugging him, and rubbing his back.

"I don't even know what the fuck happened. When I got there, they said that Kareem had been shot and had been taken to the hospital. When I got to the hospital they said he was in surgery, but he will be okay."

"Who's there with him?"

"My mom and dad are up there. I couldn't sit around that motherfucker. I hate hospitals. None of my men are anywhere to be found. Nobody's answering their phones. They know they will have hell to pay because they were supposed to be watching him, but yet my brother is lying up in some damn hospital. What the fuck am I paying them for?" He said, getting angry all over again.

Xavier's phone began ringing around 4am. He was cursing people out left and right. "You motherfuckers got 48 hours to get these nigga or else that's y'all asses!" he screamed into his cell.

Déjà went into the living room where Xavier was leaned against the wall with his head back. She grabbed his hand and led him into the bedroom. Déjà undressed him and got him settled under the covers. She lay next to him with her arms draped across his abdomen.

"Thanks for being here, baby. I'm sorry for all of this. I just wanted to be with you tonight," he said, pulling her close to him.

"It's okay, stay as long as you like," she said, kissing his chest.

––––––––––

Déjà called off the next day. She let Xavier sleep in. She went into her home office to finish up the paperwork on her desk. She got done around three that afternoon. Xavier was still sleeping, so she threw a load in the washer. She heard the phone ring, and she went back into her office to answer it.

"Hello," she answered.

"What up, baby?" asked the male on the other end of the line.

"Who is this?" Déjà asked agitated.

"Oh you forgot my voice? It's Shawn."

"You got a lot of nerve calling my house. How the hell did you get my number anyway?"

"Your cousin gave it to me."

"Wait until I see that trick," she said under her breath. "Don't call my house anymore."

"Oh, that's how it is?"

"Yeah, now please don't call me again."

"Fuck you then, bitch, there's plenty of pussy out here!" he said, practically yelling.

"Well go get some then, you trifling motherfucker!" She said before hanging up.

Déjà sat at her computer as she thought back to the day she walked in on him fucking her cousin and got pissed all over again. It wasn't so much Shawn's call that disturbed her. When she thought about what he did, she would often think back to the night her mom caught her dad in bed with his secretary. Déjà tried hard to forget about that night, but she couldn't. She began tearing up as she stared at the floating fish that was on her screensaver.

Xavier walked in the room as she was wiping her tears away. "What's wrong, baby?" Xavier asked, noticing that her eyes were red.

"Nothing, how are you holding up?" Déjà said, trying to change the subject.

"There is something going on with you. You wake up in cold sweats for one, and then I walk in here and you're crying. Now, tell me what's up," he said, pulling her up, taking her seat, and pulling her down on his lap.

Déjà told him all about the night her mom caught her father in bed with his secretary in their house. She told him how she witnessed Charlotte murder James, his secretary, and then turn the gun on herself.

"That's when I moved with my grandmother. I was only ten years old. Did she not think about me?" Déjà questioned as she cried uncontrollably.

"Is that what you dream about?" he asked, looking into her eyes.

"Yes. I dream about it sometimes, and the dreams still seem so real. It's like I'm reliving that night all over again," Déjà said with her head hung.

"Is that why you have a hard time trusting men?" He said, rubbing his hands through her hair.

"Yeah, and the fact that every man I've ever dated cheated on me. Are there any faithful men left in the world?" she asked, forgetting she was talking to a man.

"You're looking at one, and it's not just men, women do it as well," he said, massaging the nape of her neck.

"That's true, but I don't understand how you can claim to love someone but have no problem sleeping with someone else. That's not love if you ask me," she said, looking him in the eye.

"You're right, it's not."

"Have you ever cheated?"

"I've only been in two real relationships, and no I have never cheated, but they both cheated on me," he said.

You mean to tell me that you only slept with two women and you're 29?" She asked, not believing him.

"No, I didn't say that. I said I've only been in two *real* relationships. The others were just women I was fucking at the time."

"Is that what I am, someone you're just *fucking*?" She asked, getting off his lap.

"Nah, baby, you are definitely the real thing," He said, getting up as well and kissing her on the lips.

"Are you okay?" he asked with worry.

"Yes, I'm fine," Déjà answered and then left out her office, heading toward the bedroom.

"I'm going to go check on my brother, do you want to come with me?" Xavier asked.

"Of course," she said, getting in the shower with him on her tail.

~Eleven~

"You are approximately five weeks pregnant," said Dr. Keeler.

Jade was not happy. She wasn't ready for kids. She had so much she wanted to do before starting a family. Jade wanted to be married before she had kids, but she didn't believe in abortion.

Jay was ecstatic. He understood why Jade was not too pleased with the results of the pregnancy test, but he planned to change that. He went shopping for an engagement ring the next day.

"I have dinner reservations for 5:30 tonight. Can you be dressed by 4:00?" asked Jay.

"Sure babe, who are the other two people that will be joining us?" she asked.

"Xavier and Déjà will meet us there."

"Okay, I'll see you at 5:30," she said, trying to get in a nap.

"No Jade, I said the reservation is for 5:30, so I'll be there to pick you up at 4:00."

"Okay, fine. I'm going to take a quick nap," she said, climbing into bed.

"That's cool, but please be up and dressed by 4:00 Jade!" he said not wanting his plans to be ruined.

"Okay, I will. Bye!"

"One," he said, pulling into his garage.

———————

Jade didn't understand why they say "morning sickness". It's three o'clock in the afternoon and she was hovered over the toilet, vomiting. She looked terrible. Her hair was all over her head and her face was flushed. She felt horrible, but she tried to get dressed and pull herself together. Jay walked in while Jade was standing in the mirror, putting the finishing touches on her hair and makeup.

"What up baby, how are you feeling?" He asked, kissing her on the cheek.

"Besides the fact that I've been throwing up all day, I'm fine," she said in a sarcastic tone.

"You think you will be okay going out?"

"Yeah, I'll be okay. I've been looking forward to seeing Déjà. I haven't seen her in weeks."

He heard the hurt in her voice and saw the tears forming in her eyes. He stared at her. She felt her heart getting heavy. She wasn't happy at all about the pregnancy, but she didn't want to hurt Jay by telling him that she was considering abortion. She began to tear up.

"Jade, why are you crying?" he asked.

"No reason, Jay. I'm just emotional that's all."

"Now we both know that's bullshit!" he said with anger in his voice.

"Why are you getting so angry?" she said, with tears now flowing down her cheeks.

"Because I know what this is all about," he replied.

He turned her around so that she was face to face with him. She couldn't look at him. "Jade, you can't even look at me. You're that disappointed about having my baby, huh?"

"It's not that, Jay. I just wanted to do it the right way. I'm not disappointed in you, I'm disappointed in myself because I let it happen."

"Baby, you shouldn't be. I told you I was going to do this your way, so just let me do me, okay?" he asked, lifting her chin and making her look him in the eye.

"Okay," she replied.

"Wipe those tears away. You know I hate to see you cry."

He kissed her on lips. "I love you, baby. Trust me, I'm going to make you happy if it kills me."

"I love you too!"

"Well, with that said, let's get going. We can't be late."

They boarded the *Heart of Chicago* just as they were closing the doors. They spotted Déjà and Xavier over at a table near the dance floor.

"Hey girl," Déjà said, hugging Jade.

"What up, cuz!" said Jay, giving Xavier daps.

"You sure you ready for this?" Xavier whispered in Jay's ear.

"Yeah man, I love her with every piece of me, dawg, and she is about to be the mother of my child. I have to make an honest woman out of her." he said, mugging Jade.

"I hear you. The way things are going between me and Déjà, I might be next," Xavier said, smiling at Déjà.

"Yeah?"

"Yeah man. She's every man's dream,"

"We're going to the ladies room, so please order me an Amaretto Sour," said Jade, interrupting their men talk.

"I don't think so, Jade. You can have a cranberry juice," Jay said, kissing Jade on the forehead.

"Order me the same," Déjà said to Xavier.

They walked into the ladies room. Déjà was ready to jump down Jade's throat about not telling her about the pregnancy.

"I heard Jay say that you couldn't have any liquor and there's only one reason a man would stop his woman from having an alcoholic drink, and that's if she's pregnant," Déjà said, staring at Jade with her hands on her hips.

"I didn't want to tell anyone because I'm not sure if I'm going to keep it," she said, taking a seat on the bench.

"What do you mean you don't know if you're going to keep it? Since when have you started believing in abortions?" Déjà asked as she sat down next to Jade.

"I don't, but you know I wanted to be married before I had kids," she said with tears in her eyes.

"Did you share this information with Jay?" asked Déjà, handing her a Kleenex.

"Yes, I did. To be honest, I think he got me pregnant on purpose."

"There's no such thing, unless you're screaming rape, and I know that's not the case," said Déjà.

"Of course not, I want to have his baby, but I want to be married first or at least engaged."

"Whatever you decide, you know I got your back girl," said Déjà, already knowing what Jay had planned for the night.

"Thanks girl!" Jade hugged her.

Déjà and Jade were in the mirror fixing their hair when an older lady walked into the bathroom.

"Are you two ladies okay in here?" the older lady asked.

"Yes, ma'am, we're fine," they answered with a smile.

"Oh, okay your husbands asked me if I could check on you two," she said.

"They sent you in here to check on us?" they asked with their hands on their hips.

"I was already on my way in, so they asked me to make sure you girls were okay," she said.

"So overprotective!" they said, laughing.

"Yes, Lord! Oh and congratulations baby!" said the older lady, smiling at Jade.

"Congratulations for what?" Jade asked curiously.

"On the bundle of joy," she said, pointing at Jade's belly.

"How do you know," Jade asked through squinted eyes.

"Aw, baby, I'm old school. I know the pregnancy glow when I see it," she said before exiting the restroom.

For the first time since her doctor's appointment, Jade actually felt happy about the pregnancy.

It was something about the old woman that made her smile. They exited the bathroom and headed back to the table.

"Are you okay, baby?" asked Jay, standing and pulling the chair out for Jade.

Xavier did the same.

"Yeah, I'm fine," she said, sitting and then sipping on her cranberry juice.

They ate, talked, and laughed about their past. Déjà and Jade were reminiscing on their college days where they met. Jay and Xavier had childhood stories on one another. The band was on fire. They decided to hit the dance floor. They were now playing "When a Man a Loves a Woman".

Jay and Jade were all over each other.

"This one is especially for Jay and Jade," said one of the band members.

Jade was surprised, but before she could question Jay about what was going on, he was down on one knee. The people on the dance floor stepped back, giving them room.

Déjà was in tears. Jade was holding her chest when Xavier walked up and handed Jay a red velvet box. He opened the box, exposing a six carat, princess cut engagement ring. Several of the women had tears of joy in their eyes. Tears were now running down Jade's cheeks.

"Will you marry me?" he asked, looking her in the eyes.

"Are you serious!" she cried.

"Of course, I am. I told you I was going to do this your way. Nothing in this world matters to me other than putting a smile on your face. Will you marry me, Jade?"

"Yes, baby!" said Jade. She was now bawling.

He hugged and kissed her, forgetting others were in the room. The crowd clapped as Déjà approached Jade and congratulated her.

"I told you to just wait and see," she said.

"You knew all along didn't you?" she asked through tears and a smile.

"And you know this, man!" she said, imitating Chris Tucker.

"I'm going to kill you," she said, hugging her.

"Now we're even," she replied.

"Whatever!" She said, turning in the direction of Jay, hugging and kissing him.

"Congratulations to the both of you!" said Xavier, raising his drink in the air.

~ Twelve ~

Déjà was shaking her head and saying a silent prayer as she watched the newscaster broadcast yet another senseless shooting of a CPS student.

"That doesn't make any damn sense," she said, answering a ringing phone.

"Hey baby, what are you doing?" Xavier's sexy voice said through the phone.

"Oh nothing," she said happy to hear his voice. "Watching the news, and I'm so sick of hearing about these children getting shot and killed on their way to and from school."

"Yeah, I saw that. That's crazy," he said, shaking his head, "I didn't allow any dumb shit like that in my crew back when I was hustling."

"That's good to know," she said, blushing.

"Yeah, our only goal was to get money, not to take somebody's life."

"So you do have a heart?" she said relieved to know that he never killed anybody.

"Of course, I do. Believe it or not, I do have a very religious family background."

"I believe you," she said.

"Good. But, enough of all that. What are you doing today?" he asked, changing the subject.

"I don't have any plans. Why, what's up?" She asked, now surfing the internet from her laptop.

"My mom is having a barbeque today would you like to go?"

"Sure. Do you know if Jade and Jay are coming?"

"Yeah, I talked to Jay and he said they're going to stop through."

"Okay good, I will have someone to talk to."

"Cool, I'll pick you up at three. Is that okay?"

"Yeah, that's fine," she said.

She got up and headed into her bedroom to find something to wear.

"A'ight baby, I'll see you in a little bit."

"Okay bye," she said, and then hung up.

The barbeque was very entertaining. Mr. and Mrs. Jones were really nice folks. They showed Déjà baby pictures of Xavier. He introduced her to his brother Kareem and his sister Asia.

They were hilarious. They had major jokes about each other from back in the day. The Aunts and Uncles even joined in on the wise cracks. Asia and Déjà exchanged numbers and made plans to hang out sometime.

"Your family is very down to earth, Xavier," Déjà said on the ride back.

"Yeah I can't complain. They like you though," he said, merging onto 80/94.

"Why are you taking 80/94?" she asked, "this is not the way to my house."

"I know it's the way to mine," he said, taking her hand and kissing it.

"I've been at your house more than my own since we've met," she said, shifting her body toward his. "Hell, I might as well move in and save on the rent."

"I agree," he said, looking over at her with a smile plastered on his face.

"You so silly," she said now looking out the window.

"I'm serious, Déjà."

"We've only known each other for three months, what I look like moving in with you?"

"Why do women have to always put a number on things?"

"Because, it's usually relevant to the situation, that's why."

"Don't get all worked up, baby. I'm just saying I love waking up to you in the morning, that's all."

"Me too, baby, but let me think about it," she said, reclining the seat.

"That's better than saying *no*," he said, kissing the back of her hand.

The following day, Déjà went by Margaret's to check on her. After that talk with Gail, they had become really close. Déjà called Margaret, wanting to speak to her about her mother and father. Margaret knew the day would soon come when she would have to explain to Déjà why her mother killed her father then took her own life.

"Hey grandma, how are you?" Déjà asked, kissing Margaret on the cheek.

"I'm okay, baby, have a seat," She said, walking toward the kitchen. "Would you like some cold lemonade?"

"No, I'm okay."

"Your aunt Gail will be here very soon. She wanted to sit in on this conversation," she said, re-entering the living room, "you don't mind do you?"

"Oh no, not at all!"

"Okay, I'm going to fill you in on the things I know and the things your mother told me, but I must warn you, it could be a little disturbing, so are you sure you want to hear it?"

"I'm sure."

Gail came in just as Margaret was getting comfortable in her lazy boy. She hugged, and kissed Déjà.

"Okay, go ahead, Mama," Gail said, taking a seat next to Déjà.

"Okay, here it goes. Your mom and James met while they were in high school. Your grandfather, James father, was a vicious pimp named Money, and your grandmother Rochelle was one of his whores. She ended up getting pregnant by Money with James. When she was pregnant, Money would make her have intercourse with men that preferred pregnant prostitutes. He would charge them extra and she wasn't allowed to object, otherwise, Money would beat her.

When your father was 5-years-old, he watched Money beat, and choked the life out of your grandmother Rochelle. After she was killed, Money left town, leaving James on the doorstep of your Aunt Marlene's house," she explained to a shocked Déjà.

Marlene was a manager at a local department store. She didn't have children of her own, so she was ecstatic to raise James. When I found out Charlotte was dating James, I was furious." Margaret said, taking a sip of her lemonade.

"I knew exactly who he was when she brought him in this here house," she said, pointing to the floor. "I told her not to ever bring him around here again. I demanded that she stop seeing him, but your mother wouldn't hear of it. I didn't want my baby with the son of that bastard. You see, I knew Money. I was familiar with the life he lived, and he had done it all. I watched as Money would beat, rape, and sometimes kill his whores. He was a very evil man, but anyhow," she said, getting angry all over again, "when your mother told me she was pregnant, I told her to either get an abortion, or she had to leave this house. James persuaded her to keep the baby. He rented a studio apartment in the Garfield Park neighborhood for him, and your mother. She was seven months pregnant with you when they graduated high school. She had been accepted to one of the top colleges in the state of Illinois, but when they noticed she was pregnant, they wouldn't allow her to live on campus.

Your mother was heartbroken. She had always talked about going off to college, and becoming a fashion designer. But, just like that, her dream had been snatched away. James had promised her that once he graduated and became prosperous that they could hire a nanny to tend to you so that she could pursue her dream. Because she loved him, she agreed. She ended up staying in that apartment while he resided on campus. After you were born, Charlotte had to move back here because James had stopped paying the rent. He said he was spending all his money on books and tuition, so he didn't have the extra money for the apartment.

When you turned about four and a half, James graduated from college. I began to give him the benefit of the doubt because unlike his father, he made something of himself. But, I'd spoken too soon. He landed a job as a paralegal. He then rented himself a two bedroom apartment on the north side, but refused to let you and your mother move in with him. He would let you guys come visit on the weekend only. Charlotte tried talking to him about going back to school. He told her that he needed to attend law school, so she had to once again, put her dream on hold.

When you were 5-years-old, Charlotte found a job, working at a department store and she enrolled you in the after school program over at the Y.M.C.A, but your father made her quit. Charlotte wasn't too happy, but she quit her job, and pulled you out the program. She loved having her own money and not having to ask him for any, but like his father, he wanted to always be in control. Whenever she needed money, she would have to tell him exactly what she was using it for, and she would have to bring him back a receipt. When you were seven years old, James was promoted to tax attorney. He bought a house in Orland Park. It was a five bedroom home with a swimming pool, tennis court, and a park area for you.

He and Charlotte had begun to argue a lot; he had stopped having sex with her; he wouldn't even sit at the table with the two of you during dinner. He would take his plate in his den. Your mother called here darn near every day, crying over him. I would tell her to just leave, but she loved him too much to walk away. It wasn't until you turned ten that she noticed a drastic change in his behavior. She thought it was her," Margaret said, readjusting her body.

She continued, "I remember one summer afternoon, she decided to do a little shopping at the mall for some new clothes and romantic items. She asked me to go with her, so I did. We were in a store that sold lingerie. She was looking at some corsets when we smelled a familiar fragrance. When we looked up, there stood James hugged up with a tall caramel skinned woman," Margaret said, thinking back to that day. "They were picking out some underwear with what looked like just a string, off the end rack. I looked over at your mother and she looked, as if, she was going to faint. He began kissing the woman on her neck." Margaret played back the scene in her head as she told the story.

Charlotte approached him with tears in her eyes and pain in her heart. *'What's going on James?'* Charlotte asked him.

'Oh, where are my manners. Baby, this is my wife Charlotte and Charlotte this is Malinda,' James said, introducing the two as if there was nothing wrong with what he was doing. The woman was like, *'Oh yes, hello Charlotte, I heard so much about you!'* The lady said it in a sarcastic tone.

'What do you mean you heard about me? You knew the man was married and yet you still fuck him?'

'I have no preference,' she said looking at James with a smile.

'No preference!' Charlotte was now screaming. *'So this is the bitch that is taking your attention away from home and me? Here I am trying to find something to attract you to me again and you're in here flaunting this bitch off?'*

'Look, Charlotte, go home. I'll be there later,' he said, brushing past her.

"I damn near hit that motherfucker in the back of the head with a bottle of lotion, but I caught myself,"

Margaret said, gritting her teeth. "I tried to get your mom to move out that day, but she would. Said she didn't want to take you from your father. James didn't come home that night which made her even more upset. After she dropped you off at school the next day, she went to the grocery store to pick up some things for lunch. When she returned home, James' Mercedes Benz was parked in the driveway. She walked in the front door, carrying three grocery bags. He walked past her, and walked up the stairs.

Charlotte went upstairs to confront him, but he told her he wasn't in the mood to talk about it. She called, and told me she couldn't take it anymore, she had to go. I was so happy that she was about to leave that sick son of a bitch, literally. But, of course, she changed her mind. That was just the beginning. James began to spend weeks at a time away from home and when he was there, he hardly spoke to Charlotte. He would play with you until you went to bed then he would go sleep in the guest room. When she threatened to leave, he told her she can go, but she couldn't take you. '*You have no job or education, so who you think the courts will give custody to?*' is what he would say whenever she threatened to move out.

Charlotte had reached a breaking point. She was tired of being mentally abused by the man she loved, but no longer loved her," She said now bawling. They all were, as they relived that painful night all over again.

"I didn't know how to accept it, other than, to blame somebody."

Déjà was so upset about what was being told to her about her father and the pain her mother had endured. She didn't know any of her father's side of the family and after what she had just learned, she didn't want to.

~ Thirteen ~

Xavier and Déjà had planned the ultimate engagement party for Jay and Jade. The party was held at the *X Spot.* They booked the Latimore's as the entertainment, DJ Bricks on the mixer, and the best Italian catering service in the city.

Xavier and Déjà went shopping for something to dress in for the party. She decided on a white evening gown, a pair of sandals with a 4 inch heel, and a matching handbag. Xavier chose a white Stacy Adams suit, a Dobb hat, and a pair of white Stacy Adams shoes. They stopped in the jewelry store and walked out with a pair of diamond cuff links for Xavier, a diamond necklace, bracelet, and earrings for Déjà. The tab for everything was $17,000.

Déjà had a two o' clock hair appointment. She picked up Jade from her mother's house. Ms. Rivera was so happy that she was finally going to be a grandma, she went out and bought all kinds of baby stuff, and didn't even know what sex the baby was yet.

"Hey girl!" greeted Jade, getting in the car.

"What up?"

"Trying to get my mother to stop buying shit for the baby," said Jade. "Girl, she turned my old room into a nursery."

"Get out of here!" Déjà said, laughing.

"Girl, yeah! She is too happy about this baby."

"Well, you are her only child and she's going to need someone to keep her company in that big ass house."

"I know right!" said Jade, answering her ringing cell phone.

"Hey, baby, you still at your mom's?" asked Jay.

"No, I'm in the car with Déjà. We're on our way to the beauty shop."

"Oh okay, well I'll see you back at the house later," said Jay.

"Okay, babe, I love you!"

"Love you too, beautiful!" he replied before hanging up.

Jade had moved in with Jay soon after he proposed. He had been trying to get her to give up her apartment and move in with him for the longest, but her lease wasn't up for another six months. He couldn't wait that long, so he paid her rent for the next six months and ended the lease. The apartment manager didn't have a problem with that because she could double her rent. He had some movers to come in one Saturday morning and move all her furniture into storage.

Déjà and Jade walked into the beauty salon. "Oh shit, here comes the bride all dressed in white. Wait she's pregnant, so I got to remix this. Here comes the bride, all dressed in black," sang Neesy jokingly.

They all laughed as she approached and hugged Jade and Déjà. Neesy had been their hair stylist for the past two years. Once again, she hooked them up. Neesy would make you look like you just gotten a relaxer when you had a natural. She was just that good at what she did. Déjà and Jade got done at the salon around 5:30 which gave them about an hour to shoot over to the nail shop for a manicure and pedicure. Déjà dropped Jade off, and then she decided to go to Xavier's, instead of going way back home.

He stayed a few blocks from Jay and Jade's, so it would be much more convenient. She tried calling him on his cell, but he didn't answer. She started to turn around, but she was already turning onto his block. When she got closer to the house, she noticed Latasha's Chevy Impala in his driveway.

"What the hell is his baby mama doing here?" she said under her breath. *He didn't tell me she was coming over today, and why the hell isn't he answering his phone*, she thought as she pulled in next to her car.

Déjà tried getting Xavier on the phone again, but he didn't answer. She went to ring the doorbell, but noticed the door was already cracked.

Déjà walked in. She first checked the living room; nobody. She then checked the dining room; nobody. No one was in the kitchen either. As she climbed the staircase, she heard the shower going. She looked in the first bedroom which was Jeremiah's room, and he was in his bed napping. She closed the door quietly and went to the next room which was the master bedroom.

When she walked in, she saw Xavier's clothes on the floor. She grew angry. She walked into the master bathroom only to see Latasha standing in the mirror wrapped in a towel. Latasha looked at her with a smirk on her face.

"What the fuck!" she yelled, startling Xavier. He pulled back the shower door and was both shocked and angry to see Latasha standing there wrapped in nothing but a towel. Then he looked at the expression on Déjà's face and thought to himself, *this shit can't be happening*. He knew Latasha wanted him back, but he didn't think she would pull this bullshit. Before he could say anything, Déjà walked out. She was livid. She dialed Jade on her cell phone.

"Hello," Jade answered.

"Why does this shit keep happening to me?" Déjà cried into the receiver.

"What are you talking about Déjà, what happened?" Jade asked, sitting up on the couch.

"Every man I fall in love with cheats on me, why?"

"What are you talking about Déjà?"

"I just caught Xavier in the shower and Latasha was in the bathroom with him wrapped in nothing but a towel."

"Latasha, his baby mama?" said Jade, now getting Jay's attention.

"Yes, his trifling ass baby mama."

"That conniving bitch!" she said now standing and pacing the floor. "You know she's been salty about your relationship with Xavier since y'all first hooked up. I wouldn't be surprised if that bitch staged that shit," she said with Jay in agreement.

"You know what, you are so right. That bitch probably seen me pull up in the driveway because his door was open and he never leaves his door unlocked," she said, fuming. I'm outside your house can you come out?"

"Come in," said Jade.

Déjà stepped out the car and entered the house. Jay was already on the phone with Xavier getting the scoop.

"Man what happened over there, dawg?" Jay questioned Xavier.

"Latasha dumb ass popped up over here with my son talking about he wanted to see me. I had just gotten back from the barbershop, so I told her to put him down in his room, because he was sleep. I told her dumb ass to wait in the living room because I was going to take a shower. The next thing I know, I hear Déjà's voice and when I look out the damn shower door, Latasha dumb ass was standing in the bathroom in a towel and Déjà was in the doorway. Before I could say anything, Déjà was out the door. I slapped the shit out of that bitch then put her out my shit, dawg!" yelled Xavier as he paced the floor.

"I tried calling Déjà, but her phone is going straight to voicemail," he said, rubbing his head.

"I swear I'm going to kill that bitch if she fucked up my relationship with Déjà, cuz."

"She is mad, but I think she know Latasha staged the whole thing."

"How you know, did Jade talk to her?" he asked, getting a little excited.

"Yeah, she's over here now," Jay answered.

"I'll be there, don't let her leave, Jay," he said, throwing on a pair of jogging pants and a wife beater.

Xavier grabbed his son, ran out the house, strapped him into his car seat, and pulled the Navigator out the garage. He couldn't get to Jay's house quick enough.

When Xavier walked in, Déjà was sitting on the sofa with her head buried in her hands. Jay grabbed Jeremiah out of Xavier's arms, took him upstairs, and laid him down in the guest bedroom. Jay rejoined Jade in the living room. They went into the kitchen to give Xavier and Déjà a little privacy.

"I'm sorry, baby!" was all he could say to Déjà.

She looked up at him with tears in her eyes.

"Jay already told me what happened, but how could you set yourself up for that, Xavier?" she asked.

"I didn't know she was going to pull some bullshit like that."

"You know she been salty about our relationship since we first hooked up, so it doesn't surprise me. But, you know I'm already insecure because of my past, so I can't handle this kind of shit," she said, getting up off the couch.

"I'm sorry, baby. I know about your past and I made a promise to you that I would never hurt you. I need you to trust and believe that," he said, walking over to her.

"I promise to be more alert, so that you would never have a reason to question my loyalty to you."

"Today is supposed to be about Jay and Jade and here we are with our drama," she said, wiping away her tears. "I shouldn't have popped up at your house unannounced anyway. I tried calling you, but you weren't answering your cell phone."

"You can come by whenever you want to. As a matter fact, here," he said, taking an extra key off his key ring and handing it to her. "Now you have a key to the crib. Use it whenever you feel."

"I guess I have to give you a key to my place now?" she said, kissing him on the lips.

"You do what you want, it's your world," he said as he began tongue kissing her.

"Don't we have a party to go to tonight?" Jade said, stepping back into the living room.

"She's right, let's go. I have to take Jeremiah to my mom's. I told Latasha she can pick him up there," Xavier said.

"Leave your car here and hop in with me, Déjà," he said before disappearing upstairs to get Jeremiah.

It was already 7:10 and the engagement party started at 9:00.

———

"Come shower with me!" Xavier yelled from the master bathroom.

"Baby we don't have time for all of that. We have to be dressed and out the door in less than an hour."

"We don't have to have sex. We both have to shower. Might as well do it together," he said, rubbing his shaft. Just the thought of Déjà's naked body gave him a hard on.

"You on some bull, Xavier because you just showered."

"Okay, fine. I just want to shower with you. What's wrong with that?"

"You on some bullshit!" she said, stepping out her clothing.

She was right. He couldn't resist her nude body. They'd spent more time in the shower than planned. Xavier couldn't help himself. His dick took on a mind of its own. After making passionate love, Déjà and Xavier rushed to get dressed. Déjà stood in the mirror applying her makeup.

"My best friend is about to become a mother and a wife. I'm so happy for her." She said, removing the scarf from around her head and letting her hair fall down her back.

"I have to be honest, I didn't think that was your real hair when we first met," admitted Xavier, now standing next to her in the mirror.

"You couldn't tell from the way you were pulling on it?" she asked with a smile.

"Hell, you still never know with sisters. Y'all be having that shit sewed into y'all scalp," he said, laughing and doing a feel test.

"You looking damn good, baby," said Déjà, stepping out the bathroom and entering the master bedroom.

"I can't call it," said Xavier while massaging his shaft. "You're wearing the hell out that dress. How about we skip the party and hit the sack?" He said pulling her close to him so that she could feel his hard on.

"I don't think so. I can't miss my girl's special night. Let's go!" She said, kissing him on the lips.

They headed downstairs then out the door. "Which whip would you like to push tonight?" He asked, stepping into the three car garage.

"How about the Benz," she said, admiring the roof. "I've never seen a car with a sunroof in the front and back seat.

"Yeah, it's nice. It's called a panoramic roof. I love it, especially when the stars are out," he said, opening the passenger door and closing it behind her.

~ Fourteen ~

Déjà and Xavier pulled up in front of the club around 9:30. The valets were moving rapidly. The club looked more like a red carpet event, than an engagement party, but Jay and Xavier were well known in the city, so no one was surprised. Xavier stepped out looking like a million bucks. The women in the line, which was wrapped all the way around the corner, were drooling all over him. The valet opened the door for Déjà and when she took Xavier's hand some of the women turned their noses up.

"Looks like the word on the street spread like a wild fire about this engagement party," said Déjà. "This place is packed already, so these people outside may not be able to get in. Isn't this a fire hazard?" she asked.

"Not yet, but I'm going to have to let the front door know that we can't allow anyone else in until some leave," he said as they stopped and posed for a photo.

DJ Bricks was killing it on the ones and twos. Jade's favorite R&B duo were scheduled to hit the stage later on, and the gift table was piled damn near to the ceiling. Xavier had to get security to carry all the gifts to the VIP room.

Jay and Jade arrived about 10pm. They rolled up in a Cadillac Escalade stretch limo. The outdoor crowd applauded the newly engaged couple as they stepped out. Jay was dressed in an all-white Versace suit and a fresh pair of gators. He had a pair of diamond studs in his ears and a diamond studded watch to match. Jade was dressed in a white 3/4 length D&G dress, a pair of D&G sandals, and a diamond necklace, bracelet, earrings, and not to mention that phat ass engagement ring.

Every woman in the city wanted both Jay and Xavier, but they were both officially off the market. DJ Bricks announced their arrival as they entered the club. There was clapping, chanting, and whistling for the newly engaged couple. Déjà hugged Jade as she thanked her for the party.

"You're my best friend and I love you, girl!" Deja said. "This is nothing, though. We still have a wedding to plan."

"Yes we do and I love you too!" said Jade with tears in her eyes, but catching them before they could fall.

She was pregnant so she was very emotional. Sometimes she would cry and not have a clue as to what she was crying about.

Déjà hugged and congratulated Jay; Xavier did the same with Jade.

"A'ight, guys enough of all that. Let's get this party started," said Jay, grabbing Jade's hands and leading the way to the dance floor.

DJ Bricks threw on "Let's get Married" by Jagged Edge. He played Jade's favorite song "Just Fine" and by the request of Xavier he played some 50.

After leaving the dance floor, they headed over to the VIP area where both Jay and Jade's parents' sat engaged in a conversation.

"There they are," said Kate.

"Hey mommy!" said Jade, hugging her.

"You look stunning, baby," said Kate, looking her over.

"Hey mom," said Jay, hugging and giving his mom a forehead kiss. Then giving his father dap.

Jay's parents Mr. and Mrs. Jones had been married for thirty one years. His mother was straight old school. She stayed home and took care of the house, while Mr. Jones worked. He worked at the steel mill for over 30 years. Jay and his parents had a good relationship and they absolutely adored Jade.

"You look beautiful baby!" said Mrs. Jones, hugging Jade.

"You sure do!" said Mr. Jones, kissing her on the cheek. "You did good son," he said, joking with Jay.

"I agree, pops, I love this woman," he said then kissing her on the lips.

"Ma, who's your date," Jade asked, looking over at the familiar looking guy. "Are you trying to get your groove back?"

"It's a surprise. I'll introduce you later, and honey my groove left a long time ago and I don't think I can get it back. Where is Déjà?" asked Kate, looking around.

"Here I am," said Déjà walking into the VIP area with Xavier on her tail. She hugged Kate and kissed her on the cheek.

Jade introduced Déjà to Jay's parents. "Mr. and Mrs. Jones, this is my best friend in the whole wide world, Déjà.

"Hello," she said, shaking their hands, "It's very nice to meet you."

"Aw, so this is Déjà? Xavier talks about you all the time" said Mrs. Jones.

"Aw, Auntie don't be putting me on the spot," he said, kissing her on the cheek.

"What up, Unk?" he said, giving Mr. Jones dap.

Déjà couldn't stomach being in the room, so she excused herself on the verge of tears. She was very happy for Jade, but as she watched the two families become so blended, she realized she would never experience any of that. She had no parents to introduce and it made her nauseous. She went into the ladies room and could no longer hold out. She sat on the toilet and cried her heart out. Jade must've known that the scenery made Déjà uncomfortable. She came barging into the bathroom.

"Hey girl, are you okay in there?" asked Jade, knocking on the stall door.

"I'm sorry, girl! Go enjoy your party. I'll be fine," She said now feeling bad.

"You can't get rid of me that easily, so open the door," she demanded.

"I just had a moment, that's all," said Déjà, opening the stall door and walking up to the sink.

"What do you mean you had a moment?"

"Don't get me wrong I'm happy for you and Jay, but as I watched your mom and Jay's parents, I thought about my parents," said Déjà, applying some lip gloss.

"I'm sorry, Déjà. I didn't realize what that would be like for you," said Jade, hugging her friend.

"It's okay, this is your night. I will be fine. I just had a moment. Let's get back to your party."

When they walked back into the VIP area, Xavier came over and hugged Déjà tighter than he ever had. "I know why you walked out the room," he said, whispering in her ear. "Can you handle this?"

"Yeah, baby, I can," she said, kissing him.

Jay and Jade cut their cake. It was damn near as big as the table. DJ Bricks called for the couple to take center floor for their first dance. The Latimores serenaded the couple with their number one single "You Don't Have To Cry" that was Jade's favorite song. They also sang "For You" and all the couples had now joined the couple on the dance floor. Jay had never had a woman make him feel like Jade had.

"I love you so much, baby!" said Jay, whispering in her ear. "I promise you, the world is yours."

"I love you too, Jay!"

Kate walked up as DJ Bricks asked for the guests to clear the dance floor.

"I can't express how proud I am of you," she said, taking Jade's hand. "You are every mother's dream daughter. You're young, beautiful, and smart. I know you have everything a woman can ever dream of having. But I believe there's one thing missing." Jade was now shaking because Jade had always told her mother that her father was the only thing missing in her life and she couldn't wait to fill that hole. "There is someone here that is dying to meet you and to be a part of this chapter in your life."

Kate said, holding her hand out. The guy that was in the VIP area walked up and took Kate's hand. "Jade I want you to meet your father."

Jade became hysterical. She hugged her father so tight. "When did you get out?" she said with a smile. "I feel so stupid, I should have known it was you, I look just like you," she said, smiling at him.

"You sure do. You actually look like your Aunt Celeste," Reginald said, wiping away his tears.

There wasn't a dry eye in the building. She hugged and thanked her mother. Jay, Déjà, and Xavier came over and introduced themselves to Reginald.

Jay and Jade checked into *The Four Season's* hotel after the party. She was so happy to finally meet her father.

"Did you know about my father being there tonight?" she asked Jay.

"Yes, I did. This was my first time meeting him, but your mom told me she was going to bring him," he said while running water in the Jacuzzi. "I wanted to make this a special night for you, so I told her it would be a good idea to reunite you two tonight."

"Well, thank you, baby! This was definitely a night I will always remember."

"You're welcome. You know nothing makes me happier than to see you smile," he said, kissing her neck.

He unzipped her dress and let it drop to the floor. He unsnapped her bra and laid her down on the king size bed. He stripped out of all his clothing, lifted her legs up on his shoulders, and dove into her wetness.

"Relax, baby," he said.

He tongue kissed her clit, causing her to moan and squirm. He stuck his tongue into her opening and sucked her clit all at once. She was now trying to get away. He pulled her back down.

"I can't take it!" she moaned.

"Aw, this is nothing baby!" he said, reaching over and pulling a bottle out of the night stand.

He poured the thick liquid over her body. He licked every inch of her until the strawberry liquid was gone. He slid two fingers into her opening and sucked on her clit.

"Okaaaay…baby. It…feel...too… good!" she said trying to get up, but he made her take it.

When she started scratching, he let her up. She slobbered him down. He threw her legs over his shoulders and pounded deep into her until their bodies trembled. She could barely move, so he picked her up and carried her over to the Jacuzzi where they went for round two, three and four.

~ Fifteen ~

Jade called up her father as soon as they walked in the front door, to set up a dinner date.

She was so excited. Her mother had always told her how good of a man her dad was and how happy he was when Kate got pregnant with Jade, but he had been a street dude. He couldn't find a steady job after he graduated high school, so he had become a dope dealer. Soon after, he had gotten so stressed that he started using his own product. One day, he had fallen asleep on a friend's couch. His friend had taken his gun and murdered someone with it. He had no clue that incident ever took place until he was pulled over one day. The cops found the gun in the glove box.

When they ran the serial number, it came back to him.

They told him that the weapon was used for a murder. He was sentenced to 15 years in prison. Reginald and Kate had agreed that Jade would never see her father caged up like an animal. It was hard for him not seeing his only daughter grow up, and he couldn't stomach not being able to see her when he wanted to. Kate had sent him pictures on a regular, so he saw her as she grew. Before he got locked up, Jade was the most spoiled kid in the neighborhood. Every new LA Gear or Jordan that came out, she had it. Any toy she wanted, she got. She had the best life a kid could ask for up until that point. Every Sunday, Reginald and Jade would spend the entire day at Rainbow Roller Rink. Sunday's were their day and Reginald never missed one. When he went to jail, Jade took it hard, but she eventually got used to it. He had clearly aged, that's why she didn't recognize him, but she knew there was something familiar about him.

"Hey, Daddy, it's Jade," she said, excited.

"Hey baby girl, how are you?" Reginald asked.

"I'm fine, and you?"

"I'm great after seeing you after so many years," he said.

"I was wondering if we can have dinner tonight."

"That's fine. I'm at your mom's, so how about I just cook dinner here," he said.

"Oooh, I knew mom was trying to get her groove back!" she said with laughter.

"You so silly," he said.

"That's cool. I'll be there at 7pm."

"Okay, I'll see you at 7."

"Okay, bye," she said, hanging up.

~ *Sixteen* ~

Déjà had just finished up with her last client for the day. She got changed and hit the gym. She had been slacking on her daily workout since she met Xavier. When she walked into the gym, she hit the treadmill first. Déjà liked going late in the day because it wouldn't be that packed. She would be able to maneuver around the machines without having to wait for someone to get off. She finished up on the treadmill and was heading toward the weight machine to do some crunches when she ran into Shawn. She looked at him then walked away. He made her skin crawl.

"That's cool," he said, watching her sashay away.

Déjà was stuffing her gym bag when Shawn approached her again.

"Can I just have a minute?" he asked, looking down at her.

"No, I'm cool on that. And besides, you and I have nothing to say to each other," she said, grabbing her bag and walking away.

"Why didn't you just let me explain?" he said following her.

"I really don't care why you fucked my cousin," she said. "I've moved on to someone that loves me the way a man should love a woman, so like I said we have nothing else to say to one another."

"What you mean you moved on?" he said with anger in his voice.

"You heard me, but I have to go. Take care," she said, walking out the entrance.

She started out to her car with him on her trail talking major shit, but she ignored him and kept walking. When she got to her car, she popped the locks using her remote. She got in and closed the door behind her.

The next thing she knew, he had jumped in on the passenger side and had his hands tightly around her throat while attempting to sexually assault her. She could barely breathe.

The parking lot was dark, but she started honking the horn and flashing her lights, which caught the attention of others. He must've gotten scared because he jumped out and ran.

People came over to see if Déjà was okay. She was hysterical by the time the cops got there. She made a police report and gave them a description of Shawn. She called Xavier on his cell and told him what happened. He was furious.

"Stay there. I'll be there to get you!" he said with anger in his voice.

"Just meet me at your house," she said, still crying hysterically.

This made Xavier even madder. He rushed out of the office.

When Déjà pulled up, Xavier was outside in the driveway pacing back and forth. He helped her out the car and was enraged when he saw her neck. Déjà had perfect fingerprints wrapped around her neck. He took her in the house and laid her on the couch.

"Where do he live, baby?" he asked.

"Why, what are you going to do?" she asked, sitting up on the couch.

"He choked the shit out of you, and tried to rape you. What do you think I'm going to do?" he asked, flipping open his cell phone.

"I'm not going to let you go to jail on my behalf. I made a police report and gave them a description of him," she said, walking over to Xavier. "Let's just let them handle it."

He looked at her as if she was crazy. "Jay we have a situation I'll be there in ten, be outside," he said into his cell.

"Are you going to tell me where he lives, or do I need to find out on my own?"

"I don't want you to do this, Xavier," she said, hugging him.

He grabbed her hand and took her over to the mirror.

"Look at your damn neck!" he said with obvious anger in his tone. "What kind of man would I be if I let a motherfucker sleep peacefully tonight after

144

doing this to you? Not going to happen, baby. So you can tell me, or I'll find out myself," He said, grabbing his jacket.

"I can't be responsible for you going to jail Xavier," was the last thing she said before he walked out the door.

Fifteen minutes later, Déjà called Jade to have her to try to convince Xavier to let the police handle it. Jade picked up on the first ring.

"What in the hell happened, Déjà?" She said out of breath.

"I ran into Shawn at the health club and when I didn't want to talk to him, he choked me and tried to rape me," she said, crying into the receiver. "Xavier took off, and I don't know what he's going to do!"

"Jay is with him. I just hope they don't kill him!"

"I didn't tell them where he stayed," she said as she wiped away her tears.

"It won't be hard for them to find out Déjà. We're talking about some ex-street dudes. One phone call and they will be at his doorstep."

"I don't want them to be sitting in jail over me."

"Well, Déjà, let's be serious, what did you think he was going to do? You've been with him long enough to know that he has a zero tolerance for bullshit," she said. "We know they're going to find him, so let's just pray they don't kill him."

"Yes, let's pray that doesn't happen, but I'm about to take a shower," she said, pulling back the shower door.

"Me too, then I'm coming around there."

"Okay, girl," she said and then hung up.

Déjà dialed Xavier, but his phone went straight to voicemail. She took a hot shower and threw on a pair of pajama pants and a wife beater. Déjà tried not to worry, so she kept herself busy. She was fixing herself a salad when she heard the doorbell ring. The home phone rang at the same time. She usually didn't answer Xavier's phone, but she thought it was him because her cell phone had gone dead.

"Hello," She said into the receiver while opening the front door for Jade.

"Is Xavier there?" The woman on the other line asked.

"No, he's not. May I ask whose calling?"

"Tell him Latasha called since you now answer phones and shit!" She said in a snotty tone.

"Whatever," Déjà said, then hung up the phone in her face. "Women can sometimes be so ignorant when they have no life."

Déjà made two garden salads; one for her and the other for Jade. They turned on the news just to make sure that their men weren't making breaking news somewhere.

"I told you Shawn didn't have it all when you were messing with him back in college," Jade said. "He was a ticking time bomb waiting to explode."

"I guess when you're in love, you become blinded by the obvious."

"That is true and we both had our share of bad relationships," Jade said.

"Yes we did, but I'm glad I took a chance on Xavier, although I swore I would never do his kind again, he's a great man."

"He's out the game now, so technically you kept your promise. When I first started dating Jay, they were still hustling. I must say, I used to do this every night. Staying up late watching the news and praying Jay wouldn't be on there," she said. "I was afraid of getting that phone call saying he was either dead or locked up. I was finally at ease when he told me that he made his last drop," she said, reminiscing on that night. "You don't have to deal with any of that."

"I guess you're right, girl!" Déjà said.

"So is he making you happy?" Jade asked, changing the subject.

"I don't think I've ever been happier, Jade. He is the perfect man," She said, now blushing.

"I told you. You know I wouldn't hook you up with nobody I felt would mistreat you."

"I know girl, so I guess I have to thank you."

"You have to kiss my feet!" Jade said, laughing along with Déjà.

Déjà tried Xavier's cell phone again, but it was still rolling over to voicemail.

It was three in the morning when Xavier walked in the house to find the ladies passed out on the couch. Xavier turned his cell phone back on and called Jay to let him know that Jade was at his house.

"I'll be over to get her, dawg," he said, hanging up.

Twenty minutes later, Jay was knocking at the door. Jay picked Jade up off the couch and took her home. She didn't budge. Xavier picked Déjà up and took her upstairs. He took a hot shower then climbed in bed, cuddling up next to her. She melted in his arms.

The phone rang at 9:30 in the morning. Xavier let it roll over to voicemail. He knew it wasn't Déjà because she was lying on his chest, so he didn't bother answering. The phone rang back to back. He snatched up the receiver.

"Yeah," Xavier answered with anger in his voice.

"Your son wants to see you while you lay up with that bitch!" yelled Latasha.

"Look bitch, lately I've been letting you get away with a lot of shit for my son's sake, but call my house again talking slick out your mouth and they going to find your ass floating in Lake Michigan," he said into the receiver, trying not to wake Déjà. "Drop Jeremiah off at my mom's and I'll get him in a little bit," he said hanging up on her.

Déjà didn't ask Xavier about what he had done last night. She figured what she didn't know wouldn't hurt her. Besides, she knew whatever it was, wasn't good anyhow.

Xavier picked his son up from his mom around 2 o'clock that afternoon.

"Daddy, can we go to that carnival that's by the mall?" Jeremiah asked from the back seat of the Lincoln Navigator.

"Whatever my little man wants, he gets!" Xavier said, reaching back and tickling him.

"Do you have plans today, baby?" he asked as he rubbed Déjà's thigh.

150

"No, I was just going to catch up on my laundry," she said.

"That can wait. Would you like to spend the day with us?"

"Sure, why not? I haven't been to a carnival since I was his age, and I would like to get to know Jeremiah," she said, smiling at Xavier's clone.

They got on every ride at the carnival. Xavier won Déjà a big teddy bear and Jeremiah a Winnie the Pooh bear, which was his favorite Disney Character. They went shopping, out to eat at Jeremiah's favorite restaurant, and went for a walk at the Lake. Xavier popped in a movie for Jeremiah as he rode up Lake Shore Drive. Jeremiah was out before the previews ended.

"You have a wonderful son, Xavier."

"Yeah, he's great," he said, holding her hand.

"He's the only thing good that came out my relationship with Latasha."

"So what's the story on you and her?" Déjà asked as she shifted her body in his direction.

"Well, to make a long story short," he said, turning to make sure Jeremiah was sleep. He never talked about Latasha in his presence. "I messed around with her on and off for about two years when she found out she was pregnant with Jeremiah. I was in love with her, but I ran the streets a lot and she didn't like it. When I was out of town handling business, my guys would call me and tell me that she was fucking around with this person and that person. When I would ask her about it, of course she said that people was lying and was just jealous of our relationship," he said, mocking her.

"Because I loved her, I believed every word she said. Until, one day I came back from out of town from shaking a move. She wasn't home when I got in, so I called her cell back to back, but she wasn't answering. She came walking in the door a little after midnight with some bullshit ass story as to why she wasn't answering her cell. I was pissed for a minute, but I had been gone for two weeks, so I was in need of busting a nut. Let's just say while I was down below, I stuck my fingers in her and ended up pulling out a used condom," he said, gesturing pulling the condom out.

"You're lying!" She said with her mouth wide opened and her hand over her chest.

"My right hand to God!" He said, putting his right hand up.

"Oh my God, what did you do?"

"I wanted to beat her ass, but I had to remember she was pregnant which made me even madder because she was pregnant with my son, but out fucking other niggas. Of course, that made me question if he was mine."

"Well you can't deny him, he looks just like you," she said, looking back at Jeremiah.

"I took a DNA test for him when he was born, so I know he's mine, but I hated the sight of Latasha because I later found out that she had done some other foul shit, but I'll let you in on that another time," he said, exiting the expressway. "She really started acting stupid after I wouldn't fuck with her anymore."

"That's messed up," she said, shifting her body.

"Yeah, if you think that's messed up, wait until I tell you the rest," he said as he pulled into his garage.

Xavier took Jeremiah up to his room, took his clothes off, and tucked him into bed. He kissed him on the forehead as Déjà stood in the doorway watching him. She walked over to him and kissed Jeremiah on the forehead as well. Xavier smiled.

"I think I'm in love!" She said, looking down at Jeremiah.

"With who, me or Jeremiah?" he asked, taking her hand and pulling her close to him.

"Both," she said as she kissed him on the lips.

"Yeah, well we seem to have that effect on people!" he said arrogantly. "I can't speak for Jeremiah, but I love you too, baby." Déjà couldn't believe her ears. No man she'd ever dated had told her that he loved her.

They took a hot and steamy shower and for the first time, they made love. It was now more than just sex. Their mind, spirit, and soul were now mutually connected. That night gave them a feeling that neither of them had ever felt before. It was official. They were indeed in love with one another.

~ Seventeen ~

It was two in the morning when the house phone began ringing off the hook, Jay snatched it up.

"This better be good!" Jay said into the receiver in a sleepy tone.

"I'm sorry to be calling so early in the morning, but I really need to speak to Jade," Reginald said into the phone.

"Is everything okay, Reginald?" asked Jay, sitting up.

"No. When I came in from work I found Kate unconscious on the kitchen floor," he was now panic-stricken.

"What! Did you call an ambulance?" he said, getting up and waking Jade.

"Yeah, they just took her to the hospital. I'm following them as we speak," said Reginald.

"Okay man, we'll be right there," he said, hanging up.

"What's going on, Jay?" asked Jade.

"Throw on some clothes, baby. That was your pops; he said that he walked in the house and found your mom unconscious."

"WHAT!" She yelled. She jumped up, threw on some clothes, and raced out the front door with Jay on her trail. He jumped in on the passenger side just in time.

"Slow down, Jade! You're going to kill us," shouted Jay.

Jade ignored him and punched it all the way to the hospital. When they walked in the emergency room, Reginald was sitting in the far corner of the waiting room. Cathy was sitting next to him, holding his hand. Jade hugged both Grandma Cathy and her dad before taking a seat, Jay sat next to her.

"Daddy, what happened?" Jade asked with tears in her eyes.

"I don't know, babygirl. When I came home she was unconscious on the kitchen floor," he said with tears in his eyes as well. "I called 9-1-1 and tried CPR, but honestly I don't think I was doing it right. When the paramedics arrived they administered CPR and they were able to revive her, but they still needed to bring her here to run some tests."

"So she is conscious now?" she asked with relief in her voice.

"Yeah, she was conscious, but she was still kind of out of it," he said.

"Lord I just pray this isn't life threatening," said Cathy, starring off into space.

"Me too Grandma," Jade said as she rubbed her grandmother's back.

They waited for what seemed like forever for the doctor to tell them something. Jay hated to see Jade so upset. He tried everything to keep her calm. She finally cried herself to sleep. After about two hours, the doctor finally came out and over to where the family was sitting.

"Hello, I'm Dr. Gilbert," said the doctor, shaking Reginald's hand.

"How is she?" Reginald asked afraid of what the doc was going to say.

"It seems that Mrs. Rivera suffered a Transient Ischemic Attack, also known as a mini stroke," he said, flipping through his chart. "We doctors like to call it a warning stroke."

"What caused this? Does she have epilepsy or something?" asked Jade.

"Usually, it's caused by a temporary clot in an artery which causes a part of the brain to not receive the amount of blood that it needs."

"You said temporary, so does that mean the clot will go away or something?" asked Cathy.

"Yes, that's the difference between a TIA stroke and a major stroke, there is no permanent damage," said Dr. Gilbert.

"So is she awake? Can we see her?" asked Jade.

"Yes, she is awake but she's under anesthesia, so she may seem a little out of it, but you may see her," he said, gesturing for them to follow him.

They only allowed two visitors at a time, so Jay and Reginald let Jade and Cathy go in first. Kate was sitting up in the bed taking a sip of water when they walked into the room.

"How do you feel mom?" asked Jade, giving her mom a kiss on the cheek.

"Aw, I'm fine, baby. You didn't have to get out of bed in the middle of the night. My granddaughter needs you to get your rest. She can't grow if you're not sleeping," Kate said, lecturing Jade as usual.

"How do you know it's a girl mom?" asked Jade, putting her hands on her hip.

"Mommies know everything."

"Yeah, well this mother didn't know that her daughter was ill, so you can throw that theory out the window," said Cathy, mockingly.

"What happened mom?" Jade asked as she fluffed Kate's pillow.

"I don't know Jade. Last thing I remember is that I was washing dishes. I had just taken some aspirin because I had a pounding headache and then I woke up on the floor with paramedics hovering over me."

"The doctor said you had a mini stroke!" said Cathy with worry.

"I know, he talked to me. I have to take better care of myself. Lord knows I want to be around to spoil my granddaughter," She said, rubbing Jade's plump belly.

Jay and Jade left the hospital a little after seven that morning. Reginald took Cathy home, then went back and stayed until Kate was released the following day.

~Eighteen~

Déjà and Jeremiah had gotten really close over the past couple of months. Latasha didn't like the fact that Jeremiah was around Déjà. Déjà would watch him when Xavier was working late at the club. He loved seeing them together. There were times when he would come home and find Déjà and Jeremiah on the couch sleeping so peacefully together.

Jeremiah adored Déjà, and so did Xavier. He had never had a woman to make his dick hard and his heart heavy just from the sound of her name. He was used to women dating him because he was loaded and could buy them anything they wanted. He knew once he got out the game he was going to settle down with one woman that loved him and not just his money; he felt Déjà was that woman.

It was nine at night when Déjà strolled into Jade's house, turning on the news to check out the headlines. Déjà and Jade were going to meet the men at the club later that night. Jade was now six months pregnant, so she had to wear maternity clothing, but she still looked good. She was rocking a black maternity blouse, a pair of AB leggings and a pair of AB wedges. Déjà was dressed in a pair of BP skinny jeans and a BP blouse and a pair of BP pumps.

"So how does it feel to be pregnant?" Déjà asked, sitting at the dining room table.

"Like I swallowed a watermelon," Jade answered, taking a seat across from her.

"That's what it look like too!" Déjà said laughing.

Jade laughed along with her. "Aw, you got jokes?"

"I'm just playing girl, you look good."

"Oh, I know," Jade said with self-confidence.

Jade and Déjà pulled up to the club in Xavier's Range Rover. Latasha was standing outside with one of her girls when they stepped out the car, tossing the keys to the valet. Latasha was looking at Déjà with her nose turned up.

"Damn, Xavier must be pussy whipped," she said, laughing and slapping five with her girl. "That bitch could never be me though. I got the baby, so I'm set for the next eighteen years."

Déjà looked at her and laughed. She refused to stoop to her level, but she didn't know how long that attitude would last. Déjà and Jade were sitting at the bar having a drink when Latasha and her girl Sade walked up and spoke to Jade while ignoring Déjà. Jade just looked at her and laughed.

"Aw, it's like that, Jade?" Latasha said, leaning against the bar.

"Yeah it is. If you can't speak to my girl then don't say shit to me either," she said, turning toward Latasha and her girl.

"Your girl didn't speak to me, so why should I speak to her!" she said in a nasty tone.

"You don't have to speak in third party as if I'm not sitting here," said Déjà.

"Was anybody talking to you?" said Latasha.

"You were talking about me and if you're smart you would walk the hell away while you still can," Déjà said, getting irritated.

"Bitch, I'll walk away when I get good and ready to. That's what you fail to realize, I'm the one with the baby by Xavier, so I'll be in the picture until my son is eighteen so get used to my face, trick!" Déjà was trying to keep her cool, but this bitch definitely knew how to press her buttons.

"The way things look, I'll be around for a while as well, so you better get used to my face and I'm not going to be too many more bitches."

"You gonna be as many as I make you, Bitch!" Latasha said, handing her handbag to her girl.

Jade knew her best friend, so she knew that Latasha had just crossed the line by calling Déjà another Bitch. Déjà was a classy chick, but she was still from the westside of Chicago, and she still knew how to put a bitch on her back and that's exactly what she did.

Jay and Xavier were finishing up some paperwork that was faxed over earlier about an upcoming event. After agreeing on the entertainment for ladies night, Jay grabbed two glasses from his personal bar and a bottle of Remy Martin.

"We've done so much shit in the past, dawg. We done had pussy after pussy and here we are settling down with just one woman. Who would have thought?" said Jay, handing Xavier a cigar and a glass filled to the rim.

"I hear you man, but dawg, a woman like Déjà don't come along every day," said Xavier.

"Sounds to me like it's getting serious?"

"Yeah man I'm falling in love with her."

"Is this the same dude that was calling me a chump when I fell for Jade?" Jay asked, flopping down on the sofa in his office.

"Yeah, not only is she beautiful and have a banging body, she's educated, man, and she treats me like royalty. Not to mention, she loves my son and he adores her," he said. "She's definitely wifey material."

"Oh shit, dawg, you thinking about popping the question?"

"It has crossed my mind," he said with a smile.

"What you going to do about Latasha?" asked Jay. "Old girl is off the chain, cuz. You know she really gonna trip if you marry her."

"Fuck her! I'm still pissed about that stunt she pulled back at the crib. She lucky I let her dumb ass breathe after that," he said, getting angry all over again. "She's no longer allowed at my crib. I told her to drop my son off at my mother's and I'll get him from there from now on," he said, walking over to the one way window.

"I hear you man. I'm trying to figure out how to deal with Mona without catching a case. I know Déjà told you about her spray painting *bitch* on Jade's front door a while ago? Jade was pissed at me for about a week."

"Yeah, and shit is about to really hit the fan, dawg." Xavier said, looking out the window over the bar. "Oh shit, come on man!" he said, running toward the elevator.

"What's going on, X?" asked Jay, jumping up after Xavier.

"Dawg, Déjà just knocked the shit out of Latasha," said Xavier as he banged on the down button.

"Get over to the bar now!" Jay yelled to security through the walkie-talkie.

The security guard pulled Déjà off of Latasha just as Xavier and Jay were approaching the bar. Jade then kicked Latasha while she was trying to get up off the floor.

Déjà was fuming. She tried to ignore Latasha and her jealous streak, but she hated to be constantly tested. Latasha's face was swollen and her bottom lip was bleeding from the whooping that Déjà had put on her.

"Jade, are you riding with me or Jay, because I'm out of here. I don't have time for this dumb shit," she said, snatching away from Xavier and heading for the exit.

Xavier was furious because he knew that Déjà was pissed. He had never seen her that angry and he didn't like it, but he knew it was his fault.

"Don't call me until you can learn to control your damn women. I'll park your car in your driveway," Déjà said to Xavier before getting into the car and pulling off.

"I warned that bitch," he said, looking around for Latasha.

He found her coming out the ladies room. Xavier grabbed her by the throat and lifted her off her feet. "I told you what was going to happen if you kept pressing my buttons didn't I?" He said, choking her.

Jay grabbed Xavier.

"This is not the place, X. we'll get this bitch another time!" he said, prying Xavier hands from around her neck.

Latasha fell to the floor gasping for air.

"I'm not done with you," he said in her ear. "You think Déjà fucked you up, wait until I get done with you. Get this bitch out my spot before I kill her," Xavier said to security.

~ Nineteen ~

Jade was already tired of being pregnant. Jay waited on her hand and foot. He helped out with the household chores, while still trying to hold down the club and his other businesses.

Jay and Jade were on their way out to catch a movie when his cell phone rang. He ignored the call, then powered it off. He wanted to spend the day with Jade with no disturbances. After the movie, he took her out to dinner and for cheesecake at her favorite spot. He took her for a walk on the beach. It was a little after midnight when they returned home. He powered his phone back on and threw it on the kitchen counter.

Jade had gone into the bathroom to run a tub of water when she heard a big bang. She ran down the stairs only to see two men standing there dressed in black ski masks and the biggest gun she had ever seen.

"Go back upstairs, baby," said Jay, standing there with his hands in the air.

"No, I'm not leaving you," she said, walking down the stairs.

"Jade get back upstairs!" he yelled at her.

"Naw, bitch, come on down here," the shorter guy demanded.

"Calm down dude. This chick is fine!" said the taller one, "And, she pregnant! You know they say pregnant pussy is the best kind. I'm going to have to hit that before we leave this motherfucker."

"Man, what the hell y'all want?" Jay asked through gritted teeth.

"What you think we want, high roller?" the shorter one said.

Jay knew that these dudes were not only scared, but they were young. He looked over at a scared Jade who was now standing next to him.

"Next time I tell you to do something, you need to listen," he said in a whisper.

"Shut the fuck up!" The taller guy demanded.

"Where the fuck is the money?" said the shorter guy.

Jay knew he recognized that voice, but he couldn't figure out where he had heard it. "The loot is in the basement," Jay said still trying to put a face to the voice.

"You're going to take me to the money," said the shorter one, pointing the gun at Jay. "My brother can take care of business with old girl just in case you try something slick."

Those words alone made Jay's blood boil. *Apparently, these nigga's don't know who the hell I am if they thought they were going to run in my crib and walk out,"* Jay thought to himself.

Jay looked over at Jade who now had tears flowing down her face. Jay leaned over and kissed Jade on the cheek. "Don't cry, baby, you know I'm not going to let anything happen to you," he said in a whisper.

The taller guy grabbed Jade and pushed her in the living room then pushed her down on the couch.

The shorter guy ordered Jay to walk toward the basement door with the nose of the gun pressed into his back. Jay walked down the dark basement stairs with the short guy right on his trail. He could hear things being knocked around and the muffled screams of his fiancée.

"I know you got a light in this bitch?" said the short guy. "Yeah man it's at the bottom of the stairs," said Jay.

When Jay got to the bottom of the stairs he reached over to hit the switch, but also grabbed his glock off the shelf right next to it. Before the short guy could react, Jay had let one round off in his head.

He picked up the guy's gun and sprinted up the stairs where he now heard complete silence. When he walked into the living room the taller stick up kid was unzipping his pants and Jade was lying on the couch motionless. He was positioning himself between her legs when he felt the cold steel on the back of his head.

"Get your punk ass up!" Jay said not taking his eyes off of him.

"Be cool, Jay. I'm sorry, please don't shoot me!" the taller stick up kid begged.

"Turn around and take off that motherfucking mask," Jay demanded.

The kid did as he was told. To Jay's surprise, the stick up kid was indeed a kid. It was Mona's little brother Montrell.

"I'm sorry man. My sister made us do it," he confessed.

"Who is the other dude downstairs with a slug in his head? Please don't tell me it's your other brother Maurice!" he asked.

"Yeah man, it's him."

Jay didn't know what to do. *I watched these boys grow up, and now Mona dumb ass done sent them in my crib to rob me,"* he thought.

"Ain't this some shit," he said.

He tried to rape my baby. I can't let him walk out of here, he thought to himself before pulling the trigger.

He looked down at Jade and noticed that the entire right side of her face was battered. Montrell had knocked her unconscious.

"Wait until I catch that bitch!" he said to himself.

That was the difference between Jay and Xavier. Jay was quick on the trigger. He shot first and asked questions later. He looked down and saw that Jade was bleeding between her legs. He grabbed the cordless off the end table and dialed 9-1-1.

~ Twenty ~

Déjà had ignored all of Xavier's calls, flowers, and cards for the past two weeks. She couldn't deal with the baby mama drama. She had tried everything to avoid the situation that went down that night. Déjà loved and treated Jeremiah as if he was her own flesh and blood, but that still wasn't enough.

Déjà knew what the disrespect from Latasha was all about. She still wanted Xavier and was pissed because she was with him. Xavier had called so much that Déjà had to turn off her ringer. She was finally able to catch up on some laundry that was piled up to the ceiling. Her house was still clean since she hadn't been there. She was practically living at Xavier's so she was hardly home to mess up anything.

Déjà was just stepping out the shower when she heard the doorbell. She threw on a pair of pajamas and tip toed to the door. She was not ready to face Xavier. She looked through the peep hole and was relieved to see that it was Jade. She opened the door only to see Jade standing there with a teddy bear and a box of chocolate. The teddy bear was holding a heart that said 'I miss you'.

"Well hello to you too!" Jade said, walking in and closing the door behind her.

"Hi Jade," she said, flopping down on the couch. "What's with the teddy bear and candy?"

"You already know Xavier sent this stuff over through me because he said that you won't talk to him," Jade said, sitting across from Déjà.

"I have nothing to say to him," said Déjà.

"Why are you so angry at him? It's not his fault he has an ignorant baby mama."

"Because she's free to do whatever she wants to do, and he lets her."

"He can't stop her from being ignorant."

"You right, but if I delete myself from the situation, I wouldn't have to deal with it."

"I bet that chick is sitting back laughing right now."

"Yeah, I bet she wasn't laughing when her face was swollen. I gave her dumb ass exactly what she deserved."

"I'm just saying Déjà, you're giving her what she wants by cutting off a good man that she wishes she had."

"I don't have time for the bullshit that ol' girl is on."

"I hear you girl, but I don't think you should give up on him because of Latasha. That's just my personal opinion, we're all entitled to them. I could have given up on Jay for that bullshit Mona pulled, but I had the last laugh. If I would have lost my baby though," Jade said, getting angry all over again, "I would have found that bitch my damn self. Her ass would've been six feet under just like her brothers."

"I don't understand why she would send her little brothers in y'all house knowing that Jay wouldn't let them walk out," Déjà said, shaking her head. "Heartless!"

"These women don't give a shit as long as they get what they want," Jade said, concurring with Déjà.

"I'm not going to lie, girl, I miss him like crazy, but I just can't deal with all that drama that his baby momma is causing."

"I hear you Déjà. You're my best friend and I will support any decision you make, but I think you should at least talk to him and tell him how you feel," she said, opening the box of chocolate.

Déjà didn't respond. She hugged the teddy bear and thought about what her friend was telling her. They sat and talked for about an hour when Jay called and asked Jade if she would come home and watch a movie with him. Déjà turned her ringer on as soon as Jade left. She called Xavier and asked him to come over so they can talk. He didn't hesitate. He was ringing the doorbell twenty minutes later.

"What, were you sitting outside my house?" She asked, opening the door.

"Actually, I was on my way home from my barbershop when you called, but I'm glad you did," he said, walking in and closing the door behind him.

"Only reason why I called you is because I felt I at least owe you an explanation as to why I decided to end our relationship," she said, taking a seat on the sofa.

"So you decided to end our relationship?" he said, sitting across from her so that he can look her in the face. "I have no say so in this decision?"

"No, not really, Xavier."

"Okay, why are you doing this, Déjà?"

"Xavier, I had enough pain in my life and I'm tired of heartache. Nothing in my life has ever worked out in my favor," she said, picking up and hugging a couch pillow. "Let's keep it real, Latasha will never let us be happy because she still wants you."

"You know I don't want to cause you any pain, baby, but don't let her do this to us Déjà." He stood up, walked over, and took a seat next to her.

"You say you don't want to cause me any pain but what do you think you're doing Xavier?" she said in a firm tone.

"I will admit that I let my guard down, but I promise you it will never happen again babe," he said putting his arm around her and pulling her close to him. "Please don't give up on me Déjà."

"Xavier you know that I love you, but how do I know that I can trust you? Every time I turn around your baby momma is fucking with me. She doesn't even know me. We both know her reasoning for the bullshit, and that's you. She's fucking with me because she still wants you which means there is no winning as long as I'm messing with you. I don't have time for this kind of drama."

"Just trust me, babe, I will handle her," he said. "I don't want to lose you."

"I don't want to lose you either, Xavier. But like she said, I'm going to have deal with her for the next eighteen years and I don't know if I can do that."

"No you won't, I promise. Just let me handle it Déjà. I swear I will try to keep this as far away from you as possible."

"How do you plan on doing that?"

"I don't know yet, but just trust me!"

Déjà took a deep breath. She wanted to believe Xavier, but she knew Latasha wasn't going to stop until she got what she wanted. She looked over at him and said, "Okay, but I'm telling you Xavier, this shit is far from over. I can see it now."

"Don't worry about none of that. Just kiss me," he demanded.

She complied. "I love you, Déjà!" he said through kisses.

"I love you too!" she replied.

~ Twenty-One ~

Two months had gone by since Jade almost miscarried. She was now 8 months pregnant. They were just getting settled into their new home. Jade wanted to move after the attempted robbery. She felt if Mona tried it once, she would definitely try it again.

Jay had gone over to Mona's apartment, but she'd moved out. She knew that Jay had found out that she had her brothers to rob him and that she tried to cause Jade to have a miscarriage. When the cops got to the house that night, they checked the pockets of the two young boys for identification. They found a Ziploc bag that contained two abortion pills. The plan was to give them to Jade. That alone put an expiration date on Mona's head.

Jade was on her way to her mother's house to check on her wellbeing, when she spotted a man that looked identical to her Uncle Paul. He was sleeping on the ground outside a corner store.

"I don't know why mom won't move from over here," Jade said to herself.

She wasn't sure if that was him or not, so she kept going. Ten minutes later, she was at her mother's doorstep. She opened the screen door and walked into the house. Kate was standing in the kitchen.

"Hey, Mom, how are you feeling?" Jade asked Kate.

"I'm fine, honey. How's my grandbaby?" Kate said, rubbing Jade's big belly.

"Busy!" she said, looking down and rubbing her belly as well. "Where's Dad?"

"He should be home soon. He doesn't get off work until six."

"Oh okay," Jade said, taking a seat on the sofa.

"So, are y'all all settled into that big house y'all done bought?"

"Yeah, just about. You know Jay won't let me do anything until I have the baby. I be sneaking and unpacking while he's at the office."

"Girl, you better sit your butt down. You need to be getting all the rest you can now, because once that baby is born, sleep as you know it will be long gone."

"Yeah, that's what people keep saying."

Kate was lecturing Jade on mothering a child when Reginald came walking in. He'd gotten a job as a construction worker. One of his old school buddies owned a construction company and gave him a job, paying him under the table. Because of his criminal background, no one else would hire him.

"Hey honey," said Reginald, greeting Kate. "There's my girl!" he said, kissing Jade on the cheek and rubbing her belly.

"Hey, Daddy," Jade said.

"How is my grandbaby?"

"Kicking like crazy!" she said, looking at her belly.

"I can't wait to see him!" He said, guessing a boy.

"Her!" Kate said.

"It a boy," Reginald whispered to Jade.

"Well, we would see who guessed right in one month," Jade said, settling the dispute.

~ Twenty-Two ~

Xavier had surprised Déjà with a vacation to Jamaica. Déjà had always talked about going there ever since she had seen the movie "How Stella Got Her Groove Back". There was only one problem; Déjà had a fear of flying.

After days of convincing Déjà that there was nothing to getting on a plane, she had finally agreed to go. They checked in at the most beautiful resorts in Montego Bay, Jamaica. Déjà had never been to such a beautiful place. Xavier used to come there often on business, so he knew she would love it. Déjà didn't waste any time changing into her two piece bathing suit and heading out to the beach.

"This place is absolutely beautiful!" she said, sitting on the beach in a lounge chair sipping on rum punch with Xavier.

"It is, and it feels good to be away from all the drama and be at peace," he said, taking a seat behind her.

"I got you all to myself for the next three days."

They went snorkeling, sightseeing, and shopping, but for the most part they made love.

Xavier powered his cell on when they landed at the airport. Seconds later, his phone began to ring. It was his mother.

"Hello," he answered.

"Boy where have you been? I've been calling you for days," she said grilling him.

"I was on vacation," he said as he loaded the luggage into the Navigator.

"Vacation?" she questioned, "Latasha brought this boy over here three days ago. She said you were coming to get him."

"She did what?" he said stopping what he was doing.

"She said she spoke to you and you told her to drop him off here and you'll be right over to get him."

"I haven't spoken to her in over a week," he said opening the passenger side door for Déjà.

"That child was in the car with some thug. He had his music blasting throughout the neighborhood," she said, sounding disgusted.

"She had on this little bitty skirt that had half of her tail showing. Son, what did you see in that girl?"

"Nothing Ma, she was a mistake that I wish I could take back" he said getting in the driver's side. "Jeremiah has been there for three days and you haven't heard from Latasha?"

"That's right!" she answered. "I love my grandson but I got things to do, Xavier. I had to miss my doctor's appointment and I tried calling Latasha, but her phone is going straight to voicemail."

"I'm sorry about that ma; I'll be there in about thirty minutes."

"Alright, son, see you when you get here," she said, hanging up.

After picking Jeremiah up from his mother's house, Xavier hopped back on the expressway, heading home where Déjà had left her car. Déjà was sound asleep. She woke up as they pulled into the driveway. The street was dark and Xavier didn't have his outside lights on. After he loaded Déjà's things into her car, he kissed her and watched her get in. When she started her car and put it in reverse it wouldn't move. She tried it again and again.

"What's the matter, did you forget something?" he asked walking up to the driver's window.

"No, my car won't go in reverse," she said, trying to put it in drive.

"What do you mean it want go in reverse?" he asked. "It sounds like your transmission may be going out."

"I just got my car out the shop and they didn't say anything was wrong with my transmission," she said, stepping out and walking around the car.

"Pop the hood, I'm going to go turn on the outside lights so I can see," he said, walking toward the front door. He disarmed the alarm then hit the switch for the outside lights.

"What the fuck!" she yelled as she looked at the damage to her car when the outside lights came on.

Xavier stopped dead in his tracks when he saw the damage to Déjà's Honda, Accord.

"Son of a bitch!" he said, walking around the car.

All four of Déjà's tires had been slashed and bitch was scratched twice on the hood, on every door, and on the trunk of the car. Xavier was furious because he already knew who had done it. Déjà looked at him with anger in her eyes.

"This is the work of Latasha isn't it?" She asked, walking toward him.

"I'm not going to lie, this does look like something she would do baby, but I'll find out for sure," He lifted Jeremiah out the car and carried him in the house.

Déjà looked up and saw a black Chevy Impala parked at the end on the block. She knew of only one person with that car and that was Latasha. She walked to the end of the driveway and the Chevy Impala pulled off.

"Get your bitch ass out the car you dumb ho!" Déjà yelled as the car sped past her.

Déjà was infuriated. She pulled out her cell phone and dialed her girl Jade. She picked up on the third ring.

"What's up girl?" Jade answered, "how was your vacation?"

"It was great until we pulled into Xavier's fucking driveway and I saw my damn car!" she said with anger in her voice.

"What's wrong with your car?" she asked.

"Latasha ho ass slashed all my tires and scratched 'BITCH' on every part of my shit," she said, looking over at her car once again.

"We're around at the old house, so we're on our way over there," Jade said, hanging up before Déjà could protest.

She went into the house and Xavier had changed clothes and was in the closet loading his pistol. He tucked it in his pants.

"What are you doing, Xavier?" she said, standing in the doorway of the walk-in closet.

"What you think I'm doing," he said, now loading another pistol. "I'm about to kill this bitch. I tried to be cool with her because she is the mother of my child, but fuck that shit!" he spat as he grabbed a leather jacket off the hanger and threw it on.

Xavier was walking down the stairs with Déjà on his trail.

Jay and Jade had come running through the front door. "Man, what the fuck is up with old girl. She tore that damn car up?" stated Jay. "I'm strapped and ready for anything, what you gonna do?"

"We're both on the same page, dawg, let me grab my car keys," said Xavier, walking toward the kitchen.

"Hold up, Jay, this is not all that serious," said Déjà, trying to stop them from walking out that door. "She ignorant, yes, but that's no reason to kill her!"

"Oh yes it is, baby. Now, stay here with Jeremiah and wait for my call," he said before disappearing out the front door with Jay fresh on his trail.

They jumped in the Navigator and sped out the driveway.

"Why did you let them go Jade!" she yelled at Jade.

"Girl, one thing I've learned about them two over the years, is when they got their mind made up, there's nobody on this earth that can change it," she said flopping down on the couch. "Besides that bitch deserve it."

"She deserves an ass whooping, but not to be killed!"

"Oh girl chill out, they may just ruff her up, but they're not going to kill her."

"That's not what it looks like, Jade."

"Turn to *The Game*," demanded Jade, ignoring Déjà.

She propped her feet up on the coffee table. Déjà did as she was asked. That was her favorite show, besides; it took her mind off of what was going on. They dosed off at a little past midnight.

It was after one in the morning when they were awakened by someone banging on the front door.

Jade grabbed the baseball bat that was in the corner next to the front door while Déjà looked out the peep hole.

"Put that down girl, it's just Asia," she said holding her chest.

"Girl, why are you banging on the door like you the damn police?" Déjà asked snatching open the door.

"Where the hell is Xavier?" she questioned going from room to room.

"He not here girl, what's up with you?" said Déjà, grabbing her arm.

"What's up is, that Xavier's crazy ass baby mama slashed my mama tires on her car and I'm about to fuck her ass up," she yelled while throwing her hands up in the air.

"My mama ain't never done nothing, but tried to help that trick and this is the bullshit she pulls!"

"How you know it was her?" she asked, just wanting to etch in stone that indeed it's Latasha fucking up cars because she's a coward.

"My mama seen her doing it, but by the time she got out there, the bitch had already jumped back in the car and sped off." She said, taking a seat on the sofa. "I went to that bitch house, she wasn't there, but I'll catch her ass. When I do, it's gonna be on and poppin'!"

~Twenty-Three~

Déjà called a tow truck. She had them to tow her car to a nearby Honda dealership. Xavier and Jay came in a little after five in the morning. Déjà, Jade, and Asia were sleep on the sectional. Déjà woke up when she heard them come in. Jay cuddled up next to Jade. Xavier took Déjà's hand and led her upstairs. Déjà filled him in on what Asia had told them. He was so angry he couldn't sleep. They had staked out Latasha's crib for hours waiting for her to pull up, but she never came home.

"I never thought I would have to kill this bitch, but I guess life is full of surprises," he said taking a seat in a chair facing the window.

"No, her messing up a couple of cars is no reason to take her life," she said, sitting on the edge of the bed.

"I had my car towed to the dealership and Asia said your mom did the same."

"So what you want me to do, just ignore the fact that this bitch done blew a fuse?" he said, looking at her like she was crazy.

"Whether it's today, weeks, or months from now, I'm going to either kill the bitch or make her crazy ass wish she was dead."

"Can't we just call the cops?" she asked, trying to reason with him.

"Are you serious? I don't go to no damn cops with my problems!" He said with a devilish laugh.

Déjà thought back to what Jade had said *when they got their mind made up, there's nobody on this earth that can change it,* and so she decided to just let it go.

"Why is she doing this?" she asked. "Are you sleeping with her, sending mixed signals, or something of that sort? Why is she fucking with people?"

"No, baby, I haven't messed with that girl in years," he said sitting next to Déjà. "She been trying to get back with me, but I would never mess with her and when you came in the picture I think that really pissed her off."

"Well don't think for a second that I'm going to sit back and continue to let her tear my shit up, all because she don't know how to let you go."

"Hell, I'm not going to sit back and let her fuck with you either, but she really fucked up when she took that bullshit to my momma crib," he said, getting pissed all over again. "I should have paid attention to the signs that she wasn't all there."

"Signs, what signs?" she asked with curiosity.

"She used to say shit like 'if I can't have you nobody will' or she would say 'if you ever leave me, I would make your life a living hell', but of course, me being a man, I was flattered by that shit."

"You didn't tell me what else she did, care to fill me in, so I can try to make sense of all this?" she asked.

"I told her I didn't want any kids with her because she was cool to kick it with, but as you now know, she's not the settling down type. She would always talk about having a baby with me, so I made sure I always stayed strapped tight. One night, I ran out of condoms, but she said she had one. Afterwards, I took it off and tossed it, but I didn't think to check the trash can. A few weeks later, she came and told me she was pregnant. I was pissed. I told her it wasn't mine. That's when she snapped. She started tearing up my cars, busting out windows, and all kind of dumb shit. I let that slide and gave her another chance until she was about six or seven months. That's when I pulled out the used condom. That was the end right there. I never touched her again after that.

After Jeremiah was born, I took a DNA test for him and it came back that he was mine. I told her I would be there for my son, but I didn't want anything to do with her. That wasn't good enough for her. When Jeremiah was about two months old, I ran into one of her cousins. She told me that Latasha had impregnated herself using a turkey baster and a used condom that was filled with my soldiers. I snapped, I was raised not to hit women, but that shit she did was foul. I fucked her up," he admitted.

"I love my son, but I was still deep in the game. I was not ready to settle down with any kids, but she couldn't respect that. For some reason, she can't seem to move the fuck on. I'm trying to let the bitch breathe, but she's pushing me closer and closer to the edge."

"Wow!" was all Déjà could say.

———————

Two weeks had gone by. Latasha had not called or come by to check on Jeremiah. Déjà watched him at night when Xavier was at the club. His mother would watch him during the day if Xavier had a meeting or something.

Xavier was sitting behind his desk on a business call when his cell phone rang. He looked at the screen and ended the call when he saw that it was Latasha. He and Déjà had been enjoying Jeremiah's company so he didn't care if she never came back around. She called back to back until he answered.

"What do you want, Latasha?" he asked with attitude.

"Can you come over so we can talk?" she asked, trying to sound sexy.

"We have nothing to talk about. I got Jeremiah."

"You better not have him around that bitch of yours!" she said in an angry tone

"That's none of your business," he said, getting frustrated.

"That's my son, so that is my business!" she said.

"Your ass been gone for two weeks; It's clear you don't give a fuck about our son," he said, getting up from his desk.

"Is that you saying that, or that bitch of yours?" she said with anger in her voice.

"You are ignorant as hell! But, like I said, don't call me anymore unless it has something to do with Jeremiah." He hung up on her.

Xavier was looking out over the dance floor when he spotted Latasha sitting over at the bar. Instantaneously, he became furious because he had given his security simple instructions and that was, she was not allowed in or around the club. His cell phone rang as he pressed the down button on the elevator, it was Déjà.

"Hey baby," he answered on the first ring.

"Hey, where are you?" she asked.

"At the club finishing up the paperwork for the concert next week, is everything okay?" he asked putting his foot in the doorway of the elevator to keep it from closing.

"Yeah, I was just checking on you that's all, finish up and I'll talk to you later," she said.

"Okay, baby," he said as he stepped onto the elevator, letting the doors close which caused the call to drop.

Xavier knew better than to tell Déjà that Latasha was at the club because she would have been there in a heartbeat to whoop her ass. She was still pissed about her car, although Xavier covered all the repairs. When he stepped into the lobby of the club, the guests all greeted him as he made his way through the crowd toward the bar. By the time he got over there, Latasha was no longer sitting there.

"Hey, Pierre, where did the chick go that was just sitting here?" he asked the bartender.

"She was just here a minute ago," he said looking around the club.

As he headed for the elevator to get his things, he bumped into one of the security guards.

"What in the hell am I paying y'all for?" he asked Smoke, one of the bouncers.

"What are you talking about, boss?" Smoke questioned Xavier.

"I told y'all I didn't want Latasha in or around my spot and I look out my window and see her sitting over at the bar," he said with anger in his voice.

"I been at the front door all night, so I know she didn't come in through there" he said assuring him.

They both looked toward the back door, "She must've snuck her dumb ass in through the back door," said Smoke.

"You have to be kidding me!" Xavier said going toward the backdoor with Smoke on his trail. When Xavier and Smoke reached the backdoor they were shocked to see the door cracked.

Smoke drew his gun and pushed the door open, walking out into the alley. There was nobody out there, but he saw a black Chevy Impala sitting at the end of the alleyway. Xavier and Smoke walked toward the car to see if anyone was in it.

As they got closer to the car, the headlights came on and the car sped toward them. They both jumped inside a nearby dumpster. Smoke began busting shots at the back of the car as it sped down the alleyway turning right onto the main street.

"Man, what the hell was that all about?" asked Smoke jumping out the dumpster and tucking away his gun.

"Latasha ass pissed because a nigga won't fuck with her, but this bitch done lost her mind," Xavier said walking back toward the club.

Just as they reached the back door, Xavier received a text message on his cell from Latasha. It read: *YOU HAVE ONE WEEK TO BREAK IT OFF WITH THAT BITCH OR I PROMISE I WILL MAKE YOUR LIFE A LIVING HELL.* ☺

"This bitch is crazy as hell, but she ain't seen crazy yet," Xavier said to himself while dialing Latasha.

"I knew you would be calling!" Latasha answered in a chipper tone.

"What the fuck is your problem?" He yelled into his cell phone.

"You already know, you think I'm going to let you ignore me while you're playing house with that bitch?" She said in a tone Xavier had never heard before.

"You don't tell me what the fuck I'm going to do with my life. I take care of my son that should be all that matter!" he screamed into the phone. "I don't

206

owe you shit and I told you once before and this is the last time I'm going to tell you, keep your ass away from me and my girl or I swear your ass gonna end up in a body bag."

"Like I said before, if I can't have you, no one will!" She yelled before hanging up on him.

Xavier was furious. He had never seen this side of Latasha.

"I'm going to have to kill this bitch," he said to himself.

~Twenty-Four~

It was 1:36am when Jade was awakened out her sleep with a sharp pain at the pit of her stomach. It felt like menstrual cramps, but ten times worse. Jade screamed out to Jay. He jumped up out his sleep.

"It's time Jay!" she said hitting him, holding her stomach with one hand, and clenching the sheets with the other.

"What do you mean? You're not due for another week," he said turning on the lamp.

"Well I think she changed her mind!" she yelled.

"Okay, let's see how far apart the contractions are." He grabbed his Rolex off the nightstand.

"They're nine minutes apart," he timed. He picked up the phone and dialed the hospital.

"Can you transfer me to Doctor Patel?" Jay asked the receptionist.

"What is this in regard to?" she asked.

"My wife is in labor," he said rubbing her back.

"Okay let me transfer you to the birthing center, please hold," said the receptionist.

There was a slight pause in the line.

"Birthing Center," answered a girl with a Latin accent.

"Yes my wife is in labor and I wanted to know if Doctor Patel is in?" Jay asked, throwing his clothes back on.

"How far apart are her contractions?"

"They are nine minutes apart."

"What's your wife's name?" she asked, picking up her chart.

"Jade Rivera," he answered as he helped Jade to her feet.

"I will call her Doctor and let him know that she's in labor, but we ask that you wait until her contractions become five minutes apart before bringing her in" she said to Jay.

"Okay," he said then hung up.

Jade wasn't too happy about not being able to go in until her contractions were five minutes apart. Jade was in excruciating pain, but she took the massive cramps.

Jay called his parents and Jade's parents. He called Déjà and Xavier to ask them to come over to help him. They were the closest and he didn't know what to do. Jade screamed through every contraction.

Déjà and Xavier were ringing the doorbell about 45 minutes later.

"Sorry we took so long. We had to wait for Asia to get there so she could keep an eye on Jeremiah," said Xavier.

"How are you doing?" Déjà asked kneeling down next to Jade.

"I feel like somebody is ripping out my insides," she said, wiping sweat off her face with the back of her hand.

"Jay what did the doctor say?" Déjà asked.

"They said not to bring her in until the contractions are five minutes apart" he answered, pacing back and forth.

"How far are they?" Déjà asked, looking up at Jay. "Quit pacing boy and sit down," demanded Déjà.

"They were nine minutes apart," he said still pacing.

"Let's time them again," Xavier said, looking at his watch.

After timing them again, Jade's contractions were now six minutes apart. "That's close enough, let's go!" Xavier and Jay said in unison.

They arrived at the emergency room at 4:30am. Xavier and Déjà said they would wait in the emergency room with the Rivera's and the Jones's who were already there waiting when they arrived. After checking Jade's cervix and estimating that she was about seven centimeters dilated, she was transferred to a private room in the birthing center. After another five hours she was still seven centimeters dilated. Jay had never been so scared in his life. He sat in the corner of the delivery room next to her bed. Jade was throwing things at the nurses. She never thought anything could be this painful.

"Jade we need you to push," said the nurse while checking the heart monitor.

"I'm trying!" Jade screamed at the nurse.

"Baby, just push" Jay said from in the corner next to her bed.

"Shut the hell up, you push!" Jade yelled at Jay.

"Jade look at the baby's heart rate," said the nurse, showing her the heart monitor. "The baby's heart rate in fluctuating and that's not good."

"I'm trying to push!" she cried out.

"Push on your butt like you're having a bowel movement," said the nurse, checking for the baby's head, "I can feel the head, mama."

Jade tried pushing for what seemed like forever but nothing was happening. Jade had gotten so frustrated that she snatched out her IV. Blood shot out her hand. Jay was trying to be supportive, but

Jade began cursing him out and hitting at him. When he tried to touch her, she would push him away. The nurse reinserted the IV then left the room.

"What is taking so long to get this baby out of me?" Jade screamed through a contraction.

"Only way we can get the baby out is if you push," said the nurse.

"Can't y'all use those things that pull the baby out?"

"We only use those if we need to and you don't need them. You're fully dilated, so we just need you to push."

"I can't!" she screamed through another contraction.

A door on the side of the room opened. About five doctors began pouring into the room including her doctor. Doctor Patel came over pulling a cart that carried a lot of sharp objects. The nurses took off the bottom half of the bed and told Jade to scoot to the end of the table. They propped her feet up and raised the table so that she would be in the air.

Jay was now petrified. He had no clue as to what was going on. Dr. Patel covered himself in blue gear with the help of the nurse. He picked up a syringe with a long needle attached to it. He stuck her in her vagina area with it and she didn't budge. He stuck Jade with the needle about 12 times. Jay was still at her side.

"Aw, hell no," Jay said when Dr. Patel picked up a long blade and went toward Jade's private area with it.

The nurses laughed at him. A few minutes later, the nurse was holding a sweet baby girl.

"Where is the dad?" asked Dr. Patel, looking around the room.

"He was about to pass out, so he asked if he could step outside the door," said the nurse that was cleaning the baby.

Jay must have heard the sweet sound of his baby girl. He came walking through the door. The nurse took the baby over so he could see her. He was looking and talking to his daughter when he looked up and saw the doctor pull some kind of bloody bag out of Jade.

"What the hell is that?" said Jay. "Man, let me know when y'all done," he said, stepping back out in the hall.

Jade fell right to sleep after Doctor Patel sewed her up. She had twenty one stitches and was unable to sit up straight up for about a week. Jay felt so sorry for her. He wanted her to have his baby, but he didn't know it would be like that. He hated to see her in pain; he was really hurt to see her hurting and there was nothing he could do to take the pain away.

Jade said she didn't want any pain medicine, but she ended up getting Statol which made her drowsy. She stayed in the hospital for two days before being released with strict rules, so she wouldn't irritate her stitches.

~ Twenty-Five ~

Déjà hadn't been home in weeks other than to check her mail. She was spending the day with Jeremiah while Xavier attended a business meeting with a possible buyer for the barbershop. She took him to the park and out for ice cream. Jeremiah loved being with Deja.

"So what do you want to do now?" Déjà asked Jeremiah, taking a seat on a park bench.

"Um, I don't know," he said licking his ice cream cone.

"You know that new kid movie is out, do you want to go see that?" she asked.

"Are you my new mommy?" he asked Déjà, ignoring her question.

Déjà was caught off guard. "No baby, your mommy is Latasha and no one can change that," she said.

"I don't want her to be my mommy, I want you to be my mommy" he said with his head hung.

"Why would you say that, Jeremiah?" she asked picking him up and sitting him on her lap.

"She never take me anywhere like you do, she be having scary men over at our house and they be mean to me. She be leaving me in the house by myself, and sometimes when I tell her I'm hungry, she would hit me and tell me to get out of her face," he said hanging his head again.

"She said she didn't want me and it was my fault that Daddy don't live with us," Déjà just sat and listened. "When I say I want my daddy, she would start saying a lot of bad words," Déjà was now in tears. "I want you to be my mommy. I want to live with you and Daddy. Can you be my mommy, please?" Déjà hugged him and told him everything will be okay. She was heartbroken.

He fell asleep on the ride home, so she dialed Xavier.

"Hello," he answered

"Hey babe, are you still in your meeting?"

"Oh no, I just finished up."

"Where are you now?" She asked with sadness in her voice.

"On my way home, is everything okay?" he asked hearing the hurt in her voice.

"No, baby I just had a talk with Jeremiah and I'm annoyed about what he told me. I'm close by the house, so I'll talk to you about it once I get there."

"Okay I'll be there in a few," he said.

"Okay, bye."

"One," he said hanging up.

Xavier was outraged about what Déjà had told him about Latasha. "He isn't going back" he said.

"If I have to hire a nanny to tend to him, then I will, but he isn't going back over there."

Déjà had tears in her eyes, wondering who could mistreat their own child because of a failed relationship with the father.

"She is his mother Xavier. They're not going to just let you take him without taking her to court," she said, trying to make him think this out. "I don't want to get in the middle because I'm just your girlfriend, but I love him as if he was my own child, so I'm taking this just as personal." She said leaning against the dresser. "Xavier he begged me to be his mommy; I did not know how to respond to that without breaking his heart?" she said.

"Aww, he's attached to you!" he said, hugging her and kissing her on the forehead. "Thanks for being there for him. I had no clue he was being mistreated by that trick, but I be damn if I sit back and let it happen."

"What are you going to do?"

"Honestly, I don't know, but I do know that he isn't going back with her."

"Well, I need to get home to finish up some paperwork, but I have an idea," she said, kissing him. "You know situations like this, is what I do for a living. Let me see what I can do. I'll call you later."

~ Twenty-Six ~

Jade and Jay had been in the house since the birth of their daughter Jania. Jay and Xavier invited the girls out for open mike night at the club. Jade and Déjà were hanging in one of the VIP booths when two women walked over and took a seat next to them. They were talking about fucking some dude and how he made her cum all over herself.

"He will never get enough of this pussy…I let him hit this shit just last night," said one of the girls.

"Women now-a-days have no self-respect," Déjà whispered in Jade's ear.

"What are you talking about?" asked Jade in a whisper.

"These two ladies sitting next to me," she said, leaning over toward Jade.

Jade looked over at the two women, "oooh, I've been looking for this bitch!" Jade said, taking her earrings out and sticking them in her handbag.

"What?" said Déjà. "Who is that?"

"That's that bitch Mona that had her little brothers run up in my house. The same bitch that spray painted 'Bitch' on my damn door," she said.

"I sure did and I'll do it again!" said the light skinned chick with fire red hair.

"Yeah and next time your ass will end up six feet under, just like your little brothers," Jade said, getting up in the girl's face.

Déjà stepped in the middle of the two, pushing Jade back into her seat. "This bitch will get hers. You just had a baby, relax."

"Bitch, who you calling a bitch?" she said, walking up on Déjà.

When Déjà turned around Mona punched her square in the face. Jade jumped up and went Holyfield on Mona. Déjà and Jade kept kicking and punching her in the face and upper body until security lifted them both in the air. They were still kicking and fighting. By the time he got to the elevator to send them upstairs to Jay's office, Xavier and Jay were exiting.

"What the hell happened down here?" Xavier asked looking at the girls and the bouncers, Smoke and Bear.

"Your girls were over in VIP stomping the shit out of some broad," said Smoke.

"Mona bitch ass…she had the nerve to bring ass up in here after what she did," said Jade.

"Mona?" said Jay.

"Yes, Mona!" said Jade.

"Yo, Smoke, where that bitch at? I've been looking for her," Jay said checking his clip. "That's the chick that was responsible for them motherfuckers running up in my crib."

"Oh yeah!" said Smoke, now making sure his clip was full.

"Take them upstairs and don't let them leave," Xavier said to Bear.

Mona was still wiping her face when she came out the ladies room. She froze when she saw Jay, Xavier, and Smoke leaning against the wall holding their pistols.

"I have nothing to do with this," her friend said brushing past them.

Jay grabbed Mona by her hair and dragged her into the backroom.

"So what, your punk ass going to kill me in your own damn club?" she said with a devilish smile plastered on her face. "You're dumber than I thought!"

That pissed him off. He popped out the clip and pistol whipped her. She cried out in agony.

"You hit like a bitch," she said spitting out blood.

"Oh yeah!" he said. "You tuff huh, I guess I underestimated you," he said laughing.

He knew there was one thing that used to make her cringe.

"Smoke, word on the street is that you have a colossal piece on you," he said staring at Mona.

Her face turned red because she knew where Jay was going with this. He knew she fucked with a lot of dudes, but one thing she couldn't handle was taking it up the ass.

"Well man, I don't want to toot my own horn, but beep…beep," Smoke said giving daps to Xavier who was getting some rope.

Jay snatched her by the arm and bent her over a table. She tried fighting him off, but he overpowered her. Xavier tied her legs to the legs of the table, then tied her hands. She screamed out so that people could hear her but the room was totally sound proof.

What she didn't know was that there was steel behind the drywall. Jay lifted her skirt and smacked her plump ass.

"Aight Smoke, go head dawg, tear that asshole up!" Xavier said.

She was screaming and crying at the top of her lungs when she saw what Smoke was working with. She had never seen a dick so big. Jay snatched her panties off.

"This is what you sent your brothers to do to my girl, so let's see how you like it. You could have killed my unborn child. You couldn't possibly think I'm going to have any sympathy for you!" he said in an irate tone.

She was trying to kick, but her legs were tied tightly. She began screaming when she felt his extra-large penis on her asshole. He was about to enter her anus, when she started begging for forgiveness and crying.

"I'M SORRY JAY PLEASE, DON'T DO THIS PLEASE, PLEASE" SHE YELLED.

"Why should I stop my man here from making you use a shit bag for the rest of your life?" he was now in her face.

"I'm sorry Jay, I'm so sorry. I will leave town you'll never have to see me again. I swear…please!" she begged.

Jay and Xavier laughed.

"A'ight Smoke you can put it away dawg, I think she got my drift," Jay said, tapping Smoke.

She was hysterical, but relieved.

"Don't bring your ass back in my club," Jay said, pushing her out the back door.

Xavier and Jay were laughing so hard at Mona as they rode the elevator up to Jay's office.

Jay walked over to Jade and kissed her.

"Why are you down there fighting and you just had a baby?" Jay asked while nibbling on her neck.

"I owed her one, that's why." She said rubbing his neck.

"Let's go to my office and give them a little privacy," Xavier said taking Déjà's hand.

As soon as they stepped on the elevator, Xavier began grilling Déjà.

"What happened to your face?" he asked referring to a bruise on her left cheek.

"That bitch swung on me. That's why she ended up with a well whooped ass," she said.

"Yeah, y'all fucked her face up!" he said pulling Déjà close to him.

She tongued him down, causing him to instantly get a hard on. Xavier pushed the stop button on the elevator.

"What are you doing Xavier?" she asked with a smile plastered on her face.

"What do it look like?" Xavier said pinning her against the wall while tongue kissing her neck. Xavier lifted her skirt over her hips and pulled off her black thong. Déjà screamed out in ecstasy when she felt his hot tongue on her clit. He propped one leg up on his shoulders and stuck his tongue deep inside her.

"I'm…cuuuumming…babe," she said trying to put her leg down, but he had a tight grip on her thighs.

Déjà's body was vibrating uncontrollably by the time Xavier released her from his treacherous tongue. He turned her around so that she would be facing the wall and stuck all nine and a half inches in with one thrust.

Déjà moaned "aw baby…slow…down!" she said through moans.

"Take it baby…Take that shit," he said going in deeper.

"I'm. Cuuummming" she sang out as he pounded against her g spot.

"Come with daddy!" he said into her ear as their bodies began to tremble.

They both fell to the floor breathing hard and unable to move. Déjà had never cum that hard, her body was still trembling. Xavier hit the emergency release button as he heard his office phone ringing. As soon as the doors opened, he helped Déjà over to the sofa then answered the phone.

"X Spot," he answered into the receiver.

"What?" He yelled into the phone startling Déjà, "I'll be there in twenty minutes," he said hanging the phone up.

It was just past 10pm when Xavier and Déjà arrived at his parent's house. There were two squad cars parked in the driveway next to Latasha's Chevy Impala. They rushed into the house; damn near knocking down one of the officers. Jeremiah was crying and hiding behind Mrs. Jones. He ran over to his daddy when Xavier came through the front door.

"Daddy, please don't make me go with her," cried Jeremiah, hugging his father tightly.

"You and this bitch done turned my son against me!" Latasha screamed, trying to snatch Jeremiah out his arms.

"No, Daddy. I don't want to go," he cried, holding on tighter. "I want to stay with you and Déjà."

"Give me my son!" Latasha yelled at the top of her lungs, pulling him once again.

"You better let him go before I knock your damn head off!" Xavier said through gritted teeth.

"Okay that's enough guys," said the black cop while separating Latasha from Xavier and Jeremiah.

"Officer, she been gone for weeks," said Déjà rubbing Jeremiah's back. "She hasn't called or anything. She's using this baby to benefit herself."

"Bitch shut the fuck up! This has nothing to do with you," she said walking toward Déjà. "You took my man, but you will never take my son."

"I'm not your man," Xavier said, handing Jeremiah to Mrs. Jones.

"I see what this situation is all about, but we can't stop her from taking him unless y'all have some kind of paperwork showing guardianship," said the white cop "Do y'all have that?"

"No, we don't!" Xavier said with anger.

"Well, I have no choice but to give him to her."

"Now, I have things to do, so let's go Jeremiah," she said snatching him out of Mrs. Jones arms.

Déjà and Mrs. Jones were in tears as Latasha carried a screaming Jeremiah out the house. Xavier was furious. He began gnashing his teeth. That was something he did when his blood was boiling.

Jeremiah kicked and screamed as Latasha put him in the car. She turned to the family that was standing on the porch and stuck up her middle finger with a devilish grin on her face.

"You know man, I've seen this a million times in the last twenty years I've been on the force," the black officer said approaching Xavier, "get you a good lawyer, and get your son man."

~ Twenty-Seven ~

Jade had invited her parents over for dinner. With all that's been going on, she hadn't had a chance to really spend time with them. It was a little past 6pm when she put Jania down for a nap. She pulled a bag of chicken breasts out the freezer and stuck it in the microwave. She set it on defrost; she put some rice on, and cut up some broccoli sprouts.

She was enjoying her alone time, since she really hadn't had any since Jania had been born. She made herself a cocktail and relaxed on the sofa. Let's see what's going on in the world she said to herself while turning on the news. Jade damn near choked on her drink when she saw Mona's face on the 65 inch plasma.

"The body of Mona Smith was found in an abandoned building on 120th St. in the Roseland neighborhood. She had apparently been shot in the head and was pronounced dead on the scene. There's yet to be a motive and there are no suspects in custody. Reporting live from the Roseland neighborhood, I'm Connie Bennett back to you in the studio," the woman reported. Jade jumped from the couch and dialed Jay.

"Hey baby, what's up?"

"Jay get your ass home now, we need to talk!"

"I'm kind of in the middle of a meeting, can this wait?"

"No, it can't get home now!" she yelled.

"Okay, baby, I'll let Xavier finish up here," he said. "I'll be there in fifteen minutes."

"Hurry up!" She said before hanging up.

Jade was furious. She paced back and forth until she heard Jay's Benz pulling into the driveway.

She snatched open the door. "Get in here now!" she said through gritted teeth.

"What's going on baby?" he asked grabbing a bottle water out the fridge.

"You didn't have to kill her Jay," Jade said in a whisper.

"Kill who, what are you talking about?"

"Mona, it's all over the news."

"Mona… I didn't kill her!" he said looking her in the face.

"She was left with you, Xavier and Smoke. The next thing you know her face is on the news."

"What they say happened to her?"

"That she was shot in the head and pronounced dead on the scene."

"Where?"

"On 120th Street in Roseland," she said with tears in her eyes.

She couldn't stand the girl, but she didn't want her dead. She really didn't want her soon to be husband to go down for her murder either.

"I don't know what went on, but I do know I didn't kill her," he said walking over to the plasma and turning up the volume to hear the replay of the report.

Jay stood and listened to the newscaster report Mona's death. He called up Xavier and told him to come by the house when he left the office. Jade called and cancelled with her parents. She then called Déjà.

"Hello!" Déjà answered in a sleepy tone.

"Hey girl, are you sleeping?" Jade asked her best friend.

"Girl yeah, I been up since five this morning. I had to meet with a client at seven and I just got home an hour ago," she said pulling the comforter over her face. "But what's up?"

"I take it you haven't seen the news?"

"No, I haven't even turned on the television today, why?"

"I don't want to discuss it over the phone, so turn the news on then call me back when you see somebody familiar."

"Okay," she said hanging up and turning to the news channel.

Jade was still watching to see when they were going to show it again. That's the one thing she loved about this channel. They rebroadcast every thirty minutes. Her phone started ringing after they broadcasted Mona's murder again.

"Hello," answered Jade.

"What the fuck?" Déjà yelled into the phone.

"That's the same thing I said when I saw it."

"Did they…?" she asked but really not wanting to know.

"Jay said no, he said he put her out his club and that was the last time he seen her."

"I'm on my way over there!" Déjà said, getting out of bed, still in shock.

"Xavier is too, so I guess we can get to the bottom of this when you both are here."

"You damn right, see you in a little bit."

"Alright girl."

Xavier arrived at Jay's around 9:30, "Man do you know how this shit look, dawg?" Xavier said after seeing the news himself.

"Yeah, I do. We were the last ones to see her alive and we did ruff her up a little, but we didn't kill her," said Jay. "We have cameras to show that she walked out the back door."

"Who would have killed her?" Xavier asked Jay. "What kind of people was she dealing with?"

"That girl messed with all kinds of dudes. From dope dealers, to pimps so ain't no telling who else she done pissed off other than me."

"I know we didn't kill her, so I'm not worried about it."

"That bitch had somebody to run up in my crib, so it ain't no telling who else door she had busted down," he said pouring him a drink. "Maybe they weren't as forgiving as we were."

"That's fucked up, but I'm glad we didn't let Smoke run up on her. That would have come back on us for real," said Xavier.

"Yeah man, but I used to tell her that the bullshit she was on would get a slug in her head."

"What exactly was she doing?" Xavier asked

"Man I remember she set up this dope dealer that owned a car wash. She planted some shit in his spot because he wouldn't fuck with her, and then called the feds on him. He got hit with a nice bid, hold up come to think about it, word on the street is; he got out last week."

"That's some dirty shit. I wouldn't be surprised if she and Latasha were cousins. That sound like something she would do."

"Speaking of Latasha, what's going on with Jeremiah?"

"Shit man, I have a lawyer looking into it, but it hurts that my son is being abused and there's nothing I can do about it right away," he said getting upset. "If I report her they're going to put him in foster care and I don't want him there."

"That's not true," Jade said walking into the living room and taking a seat on the sofa. "If you report her, they will let a relative volunteer to take him until the case is done and I can't see any of y'all family not wanting him."

"I can do that?" Xavier asked getting some hope.

"Yep, Déjà know that, she's a social worker," Jade said surprised that she didn't tell him.

"Yeah, I know she mentioned it, but we haven't talked much since the incident with Jeremiah."

She doesn't answer most of my calls because she said she doesn't want to be the cause of my son being abused. She said, that apparently her being with me is what's causing this behavior from Latasha. I understand where she's coming from, but I'm not going to lose her over this dumb shit.

"I'm trying not to catch a case, but she is pushing me close to the edge." he said, getting worked up.

"I haven't spoken to her much lately either," Jade said.

"She said she was on her way a while ago, let me try calling her."

Jade dialed Déjà's home phone first and got no answer, so she tried her cell.

"Who this?" an unfamiliar voice answered.

"Who is this?" Jade asked.

"Who you looking for?" she asked with a giggle.

Jade looked at the display screen to make sure she dialed the right number.

"I'm looking for Déjà, put her on the phone," said Jade after confirming it was indeed the right number.

"I'm sorry she can't come to the phone at the moment," the unfamiliar voice said in a sarcastic tone. "I bet she will stop messing with my man now," the unfamiliar voice said before hanging up.

"JAY!" Jade yelled while running in the living room.

"What's wrong with you?" Jay asked running toward her.

"Déjà…!" Jade said, crying hysterically which caused Xavier to approach her.

"What about Déjà?" Jay asked trying to get her to calm down.

"I…called…her…phone…and…and…some…girl …answered…and….and…..said…that…I…bet…she… will…stop messing with her…man now," she managed to get out.

"I don't know where she is…but they have her phone."

Xavier and Jay grabbed their pistols and jetted out the front door. Jade called the girl, from next door that babysat for them every now and again. Then she called her mom and explained to her what was going on and asked if she could come over to watch Jania.

"My mom will be here in about twenty minutes, so here's thirty dollars," she said to the teenage girl and handed her the money.

"When she wakes up, she will need to eat and a diaper change," she said to the girl before jumping in the Range Rover and speeding all the way to Déjà's apartment.

When Jade arrived on Déjà's block she saw red and blue flashing lights flashing in the front of Déjà's building. When she approached the building, she saw Jay and Xavier hopping in the Navigator and pulling off. Jade tried entering the complex, but she wasn't allowed in the building.

"Excuse me can you tell me what happened here?" Jade asked a female officer that was standing near the entrance.

"All I can tell you is that a woman was badly beaten outside her apartment," she said.

Jade was getting light headed, "What apartment?" Jade asked afraid of the answer.

"I believe it was apartment 208," The officer said before having to catch Jade.

She had passed out. When she came to, there were three officers hovering over her. The officers questioned her and she gave them Latasha's name. The officers told her what hospital Déjà had been taken to.

Jade had called Déjà's aunt Gail and told her what happened and the name of the hospital Déjà was at.

"I'll be there," Gail said, slamming the phone down.

Jade rushed into the emergency room. She approached the nurse at the reception desk. "My sister Déjà Morgan was brought here by paramedics," Jade said hysterically.

The nurse looked over her clip board. "Yes she is in the intensive care unit," the nurse said. "I have no details as of yet, but I will go back there to see what I can find out for you."

"Okay thanks," Jade said, taking a seat.

~Twenty-Eight~

Words couldn't explain how Xavier was feeling at the time. Jay pulled up in front of Latasha's building. Xavier saw someone looking out the window, but he didn't care who or how many were inside. He was prepared for anything. As they drew closer to her apartment, they noticed that the front door was ajar. Xavier went in first with his pistol drawn. The apartment was lit up with candles. Jay tried turning on the lights, but they didn't work.

"What is this bitch in here doing voodoo or some shit?" Jay joked.

"Knowing her trifling ass, she probably didn't pay her light bill," Xavier said.

They went from room to room, but there was no sign of her or Jeremiah. They heard the sound of moaning coming from Latasha's room.

Xavier pushed the door open slowly, and walked in.

"Man straight up this bitch is crazy," Jay said when he saw Latasha on the bed butt naked. Her legs were spread wide as she fingered herself.

"Where is my son, you sick bitch?" Xavier said putting his pistol to her head.

"If you shoot me you will never find him!" she said with a smirk on her face.

"What you mean, find him?" he said, ready to pull the trigger.

"You better not have laid a finger on him."

"Whatever, you ain't going to do shit, but come get some of this good ass pussy," she said massaging her breast.

"Dawg, shoot this bitch," Jay said getting irritated.

Just as Xavier was about to pull the trigger, Latasha's phone rang. The answering machine picked up. Latasha heard her mother's voice and tried to run into the living room to turn it off but was knocked backwards by Xavier's fist.

"Watch this bitch. I'm going to check something." Xavier said exiting the bedroom and walking into the living room. He pressed play on the answering machine.

"Latasha you need to get over here and get your damn son!" Lynn yelled. "Your ass been gone for days, he keep crying for his father and if I had his number I would call him myself. If you don't come get him tonight, I'm calling DCFS on your ass," she said before slamming down the phone.

When Xavier walked back in the room Jay had her mouth covered with duct tape so she couldn't scream while Xavier was getting the info he needed.

"Well what do you know, that was your mother and apparently Jeremiah is at her house. He has been there for the past few days. So now I have no reason to let your dumb ass continue breathing," he said taking the tape from over her mouth.

"You're going to kill the mother of your child?" she said, getting serious now that her plan had crumbled.

Xavier laughed, "You really think I give a fuck about you?" he screamed in her face. "You and your dusty ass girls jumped on my girl, so fuck you! She's his new mommy," he said knowing that would piss her off.

"That bitch better not come anywhere near my son, or next time I'll kill her," she said lashing out at Xavier, but was knocked back by his fist once again.

Xavier punched her over and over again until her body became motionless.

"Let's go get your boy, fuck this bitch!"

"Nah man, this bitch going to pay for all the bullshit she pulled," he said taping her mouth, hands, and legs.

"She thought that shit was funny, wait till I get done with her."

They covered her naked body with a blanket and carried her out the back of the building. They put her in the back of the Navigator. They drove her to the hood where all the crack heads and drunks hung out. They untied her as she begged them not to leave her out there, especially butt naked. They made her get out the truck. She tried to grab the blanket, but Jay snatched it away.

They pulled off, leaving her out there for the crack heads to take advantage of. Xavier picked his son up from Latasha's mother's house then went straight to the hospital.

Déjà had suffered a fractured rib cage, a broken arm and bruises over her face and body. Xavier was extremely remorseful when he saw her lying so helpless in that hospital bed. She had been jumped by Latasha and two of her cousins. She was struck with a two by four which is what broke her arm.

After the police caught up with Latasha, she had been screaming rape, but they didn't believe her. She was locked up and charged with assault with a deadly weapon. She had a mile long rap sheet that included grand theft auto, drugs, and boosting. Her bond was set at $100,000. Xavier was the only person that had that kind of money, but he sure as hell wasn't going to use it on her.

A month later, Xavier was awarded full custody of Jeremiah. He sold his home and bought a new home that Déjà had chosen. He didn't allow anyone other than Jay and Jade and their parents over to their home, because he didn't want to put Déjà and Jeremiah through anymore bullshit. Jeremiah was happy with his new life.

Déjà was unpacking the kitchen glasses when the phone rang.

"Hello," Déjà answered.

"Is this Déjà?" said the male voice.

"Yes it is. Who's calling?"

"This is Money, your grandfather."

To stay up to date on Tajana Sutton's new releases, please follow the link below to subscribe to her mailing list:

http://eepurl.com/x6XKz

SEE YOU IN DEJA 2…NOW
AVAILABLE!

Made in the USA
Coppell, TX
11 February 2021

50130741R00150